Praise for John Mullally's
THE FIRST LADY SLEEPS and
THE FIRST LADY MEETS AZEE

POSSIBLE BEST SELLER

If you read books by Grisham, DeMille or Baldacci, you will enjoy *The First Lady Sleeps*, a White House thriller. It is an intense saga of obsessive love and extreme wealth verses governmental power. His characters are well done and the story has several unexpected twists. The author grabs your attention and holds it to the end.

—*Louise Matz, Senior Perspectives*

DENTIST TURNS NOVELIST

Much like the prolific British mystery writer P.D. James who clearly probes her characters, Dr. Mullally's characters in *The First Lady Sleeps* are faceted, warts and all. The characters create various startling plot events as the warts change the pattern of their lives. To describe the tumultuous events is to take away the drama of Dr. Mullally's ingenuity. By the end, you applaud his ingenuity.

—*Fran Schattenberg, PhD., White Lake Beacon*

BLOCKBUSTER SEQUEL

Dr. Mullally does a masterful job in making *The First Lady Meets Azee* an exciting stand-alone book for his first-time reader as well as a welcomed fix for his previous readers. The intriguing plot of this action-packed novel set against a background of medical, legal and historical issues will keep you wishing for more.

—*Louise Matz, Senior Perspectives*

INTERNATIONAL THRILLER

This sequel to *The First Lady Sleeps* tells a well-researched, globe-spanning tale as Secret Service agent Tom Gleason struggles with the tension between traditional, slow moving justice for the home-grown terrorist Azee and personal revenge for the profound damage Azee has caused. Mullally has many surprises in store, keeping the suspense going to the final

—*Cynthia P*
SKY L

iner.
litor.

A DOMINICAN REPUBLIC *Wedding*

Leads to International Intrigue

JOHN MULLALLY

John Mullally

All Novels Publishing, LLC.

A Dominican Republic Wedding
Leads to International Intrigue

All Novels Publishing, LLC.

Allnovelspublishingllc@yahoo.com

ISBN: 978-0-9837808-7-8

Finished cover and text layout:
Amy Cole, JPL Design Solutions

Printed in the United States of America

I am solely responsible for the contents of
this totally fictional novel.

www.thedominicanrepublicwedding.com

Dedication

To Darby Marie Mullally
Our Tenth Grandchild

The World is a better place
as you join our other grandchildren

I

The Golf Club of Berlin was an amiable place in the 1920's even when Germany was recovering from the humiliation of WWI and especially in the 1930's as Germany was rebuilding for whatever Hitler had planned.

Its affluent members, including certain Jewish families, had weathered the political and economic turmoil between the wars better than the general population of Germany. Interestingly enough, the bylaws of the Golf Club of Berlin allowed those who had 25% or less Jewish lineage to be members. There were a number of those who qualified, and the steady rise of the Nazi elite and their desire for a private place for their social and recreational activities enhanced the membership value of the Golf Club of Berlin for anyone seeking to curry the favor of these rising Nazi powerbrokers.

However, as the Nazis consolidated their power, some of the Club's members began to face a tremendous uncertainty, fearful that with Hitler's increasing anti-semitism they could be barred from Club membership by the stroke of a pen.

For one Berlin business-owner, Harald Katz, who thought himself more German than Jewish, the club offered business opportunities that soon became reality, reaching even to Hitler and many higher-ups in the Third Reich. The Katz multi-generational family brewery, located in Berlin, was modest compared to the many larger national breweries.

However, more importantly to the Katz family, their beer was a personal favorite of Hitler and his inner circle of friends and advisers. Harald did not want to consider how much of this high-powered favoritism was due to the brewery's free delivery and forgetting to bill for their product. Nevertheless, the Katz family had relationships in the highest level of the Third Reich, and Harald was determined, as a matter of personal as well as business survival, to maintain and indeed enhance these contacts for the benefit of the succeeding generations of his family.

Harald, to a fault, was loyal and helpful to family and friends who were not so fortunate. Harald listened to a longtime family friend who mentioned he was having increasing difficulty finding a market for his animal hides that were the remnants of his kosher slaughterhouse. For example many excellent customers such as the old time Jewish printing and book binding businesses were disappearing as well as Jewish shoemakers who could only make shoes for fellow Jews. The result was that he was left with an inventory of hides he could not sell.

Harald's wife, Gertrud, had a fetish for fine leather gloves, a pair for all seasons and extras for social engagements. So when Harald brought home a properly cured and tanned bovine hide with the pronouncement, "Here are your next dozen pairs of gloves," a new career was inadvertently started for Gertrud. Even though she was an excellent seamstress, who started working at a young age in her parent's tailor shop and then sewed many of the clothes for their four children, adapting to the supple yet thicker leather proved to be a challenge. Hoping to get the last laugh on her husband for starting her on a new career path, she made him the guinea pig for her first few pairs of gloves before attempting the more delicate feminine gloves for herself.

Proud of his wife's growing glove-making skills, Harald always wore the latest and best pair as a point of conversation when he did his personal beer deliveries to the top three or four Third Reich higher-ups, including Hitler's residence. Harald and his well-dressed driver always did these deliveries personally to insure these influential clients received the best of service to fend-off the other local breweries that would love to have this important clientele. One day Hitler's service door guard asked where Harald got the sturdy yet attractive gloves he was wearing because Hitler was always replacing his gloves after his dogs chewed them. Harald explained his wife was starting a glove making company and these were some of her first efforts.

The guard took Harald's gloves inside and returned shortly with the comment that Hitler would like to see him. Harald was flabbergasted but gathered himself as he followed the guard down the hall to a security room where he was quickly frisked and then seated at a small table in an adjoining conference room. When the door across from him opened, he quickly rose and gave his Heil Hitler salute. Hitler gave a dismissive wave of his hand indicating for Harald to sit down.

Harald knew Hitler was a man of few words, but he still wanted to mention that they had met last year at a birthday dinner for Hitler at the Golf Club of Berlin. Hitler gave another dismissive flick of his wrist, asking if he could try on the gloves. While flexing his fingers inside the gloves he said, "They're comfortable, not the rough insides like many gloves. Your wife makes these?" Harald explained his wife was just starting her glove making business and this was only her fourth pair. He didn't think it wise to tell Hitler that the leather was from a kosher cow.

Hitler, in a rare moment of personal candor, confessed to Harald that gloves were one of his biggest frustrations since he had small wrists and short fingers. "The hands of an artist," he said. His active life style required many kinds of gloves from the casual fur-lined gloves for the cold weather at his mountain hideaways to the formal black leather over-the-wrist gloves for reviewing the goose-stepping troops.

Harald immediately volunteered his wife's glove-making skills and asked Hitler for permission to trace both his hands as hands can vary in size. Hitler smiled as Harald carefully outlined his hands and wrists on two sheets of paper laying on the table. When Hitler was leaving, Harald mentioned that since winter was approaching, his wife would start immediately on a pair of sheep-skin-lined gloves.

· · · ·

Harald's business sense of success encompassed all family members. With his two sons, he became a bit of a visionary realizing that they were going to need a broader business training than he had when they would be faced with running the brewery for another generation. He sent his oldest son, Ernst, to his banker in Switzerland for enhanced business training that the family brewing business could not provide.

Ernst enjoyed the cosmopolitan atmosphere of Geneva removed from the growing ethnic and military problems in Germany, including a business trip to the Dominican Republic to visit that country's oppressive dictator, Rafael Trujillo, who had questions about his clandestine Swiss banking accounts. Ernst was fortunate because even as the junior associate on this, his first international business trip, he was allowed to sit in on all the bank-team meetings with Trujillo.

Trujillo was a gracious host to his visiting Swiss bankers. Ernst found him nothing like his public image as the ruthless murderer of thousands of impoverished Haitians who were just trying to survive by crossing the border into the Dominican Republic. Trujillo's offer to throw a lavish party at the bankers' hotel was politely turned down by the happily married bankers because they knew from previous visits these parties always involved Dominican ladies of the night. However, as the lesser of two evils, the bankers elected to accept Trujillo's offer of attending a cock-fight as his guests.

Cockfighting was a popular legal sport that provided a

recreational outlet for the lower class of Dominican society. Trujillo's personal liking of cockfighting was true to his roots as were the macabre results of the cockfights where the strongest cock survived at the expense of the weaker opponent. Trujillo met the bankers at the cockfighting gallera and seated his guests near him in the lowest row of seats with their feet on the dirt floor of the circular fighting pit. Trujillo was very animated during each match, making modest bets on either a blanco or negro ankle-banded cock with his banker guests and other patrons seated around him.

Ernst didn't participate in any of the betting action because he was extremely uncomfortable in profiting from such a gruesome spectacle where one of the cocks was usually killed to win the bet. He avoided eye contact with Trujillo who was trying to entice the bankers into a good-natured few pesos bet. Even though Ernst knew the cockfight bet was like a bet on the golf course—more about the bragging rights than the money at stake—his conscience wouldn't allow it.

With each proceeding match Ernst sat more upright in his seat, trying to distance himself as far as possible from the cocks fighting in the pit at his feet. He had to move his feet a number of times to avoid pools of blood encroaching on his new cordovan wingtip shoes. After the particularly gruesome eighth match, where the blanco cock died resting on the tip of his shoes, Ernst felt an attack of nausea rising in his stomach, so he quickly crossed the fighting pit to the exit with the one-word explanation to his boss—"Bano." Luckily, he reached the bathroom, basically a stinky two-hole out house, where he vomited without making a mess of his clothes.

He could hear the announcement of the tenth and final match of the day, so he elected to stay outside the gallera and wait for everyone to leave. Trujillo, seeing Ernst waiting by the exit, briefly paused to ask a question without wanting an answer, "You okay? Your face was blanco."

Ernst instinctively wiped his lips with the back of his hand, trying to erase the bad taste of the cockfights, and nodded he was fine to the already departed Trujillo, whom they would see the next morning for their final wrap-up meeting.

Trujillo was aware of his terrible image in the international community because of his slaughter of hundreds of helpless and downtrodden Haitians so he made an offer to the departing bankers that was out of character for him and that caught the bankers totally by surprise. Trujillo, knowing that the visiting Swiss bankers were Jewish, proposed that the Dominican Republic would offer free land to any European Jews who wanted to immigrate there to escape the increasing wave of anti-semitism brought on by Hitler's policies. The bankers, viewing this Trujillo offer as ingratiating and self-serving, nevertheless promised to take it back to a European council of rabbis for their consideration.

This offer would eventually prove fortuitous to Ernst and other Jewish families when his comfortable life in Geneva was shattered in November, 1938. Ernst received a terse cable from his father ordering him to immediately return home to Berlin. Buying a newspaper as he boarded the train to Berlin, he saw the front page lead story on the recent Kristallnacht in Germany where the windows and storefronts of Jewish merchants were broken and the shops vandalized in a countrywide outbreak of anti-semitism that was condoned and even encouraged by the Third Reich. Even though his family did not publicly practice its Judaism, Ernst was very troubled to read that 267 synagogues were destroyed because he viewed all places of worship, regardless of religious denomination, to be untouchable sanctuaries. A few rabbis were encouraging their congregations to flee Germany to find safe haven anywhere in the world that they could.

Ernst felt confidant that the family brewery business was not targeted in the Kristallnacht; otherwise his father would have mentioned it in his cable and the newspaper did not list it in their rundown of major businesses that were attacked. The name Katz was fairly common in Germany and most Katz families were not Jewish, so the family should be safe from a random attack of anti-semitism. Of more concern to Ernst were their casual friends, business contacts and fellow members of the Golf Club who were aware of their

Jewish lineage and that it might be used against them.

In a family meeting the afternoon Ernst's train arrived from Geneva, his father, Harald, presented a strategy to save the family and the brewery. The family brewery had escaped the violence of the Kristallnacht, but the synagogue where they were nominal members was destroyed after the office records were looted, so their name could be out there as synagogue members. The family doubted that the next looting episode would spare those who were only one-quarter Jewish regardless of the legal rights given the quarter-Jews. Fortunately their old rabbi was out of town the night of the attacks; otherwise he could have been killed as happened in a few other German towns. They decided that the family should immediately join the Nazi party and the two boys should apply for acceptance in the elite Schutzstaffel - SS - corps.

Getting into the SS should not be a problem for the physically-fit boys as the commandant of the SS, Heinrich Himmler, was a member of the Golf Club of Berlin and he was on Harald's beer delivery route. If this Himmler contact did not work out, Harald was prepared to use his Hitler contact as Hitler was now wearing the wife's custom made gloves and was photographed reviewing the troops wearing the long formal gloves that perfectly fit his wrists and hands.

As a last resort, Harald was prepared to rejoin the regular German army that he had retired from when his father died and he needed to return home to run the family brewery. The boys, Ernst and Reinhard, were accepted into the SS on their own merits without having to use the Himmler or Hitler connection, so Harald felt no immediate pressure to reactivate his retired Major rank in the German army. That is, until Germany invaded Poland in September of 1939 when Germany was put on a state of heightened military readiness, and Harald received a letter ordering his re-enlistment at his previous rank of Major. After England and France declared war on Germany following the invasion of Poland, Germany was at war again. There was nothing that Harald could do except try to survive the war and return home to whatever would be left of his former life.

II

The three Katz men, the father Harald and his sons, Ernst and Reinhard, joined the German military in an attempt to insulate themselves and the family brewery from possible anti-semitism attacks because of their quarter-Jewishness. They were vindicated by a decree of Hitler in October, 1940 pronouncing that quarter-Jews in the German military were to be considered as full-blooded Germans equal to their fellow German Soldiers. Unfortunately, this decree of Hitler did not shorten their commitment to the German war effort. They were committed to serve in the German military until the end of the war, regardless of the outcome.

When Ernst and Reinhard were home after completing their SS basic training, they proudly displayed the tattoos of their blood types on the inside of their left upper arms. Their mother and sisters gasped at viewing this black on white revelation while Harald, the skeptical father, could only question, "Is that a good idea?"

Ernst proudly explained the SS's logic in having each SS member's blood type tattooed under their arm, thus readily available in an emergency if blood was needed to save their lives. Obviously, it was a good idea, he reasoned.

Harald mumbled, "But it's there forever."

The father, Major Harald Katz, was at first assigned to training new army conscripts outside of Berlin, but then he was given duties on the Western front in France and Belgium to try to thwart the slowly advancing allied armies. His weekly letters home shared the increasing doom and gloom of the gradually retreating German army, and he wondered how long before Hitler surrendered to the advancing allies with the hope of saving the fatherland from the constant aerial bombings.

Ernst and Reinhard could not discuss many of the things in their SS war careers at the rare times, usually during the holiday season, when the family would be together. However, Reinhard, the more bookish of the two brothers, was happy to describe his first SS assignment. The 1939 general population census of Germany generated much information that was needed for the future population plans of the Third Reich. The local authorities were ordered to gather up the census cards of all the Jewish residents and mark them with a red J before they were sent in for tabulation. Reinhard's job as a trusted and impartial SS officer was to verify that every town and village in his assigned district met this reporting requirement. Then he would keep a running tally of the Jews reported in his district before he sent the final Jewish census numbers to Berlin.

Reinhard could detect that his father, Harald, was becoming uncomfortable with the discussion of the census where the Jews were being singled out for special tabulation, so he went on to describe his current SS assignment at Warsaw in the newly conquered Poland.

Reinhard assured his family that he had a safe desk job that was proving to be very interesting. He was trying to entrap and ultimately capture, so far unsuccessfully, a lady in the Warsaw welfare office, who was hiding and smuggling Jewish children out of Poland, when they were supposed to be accounted for in the newly established ghettos. His mother's usual warning, "Reinhard, please be careful," fell on deaf ears.

Ernst had to use extreme discretion in describing his jobs in the SS to his family and friends. His SS training instructed him to blindly follow orders and certainly not to discuss any required actions with anyone, even family or fellow SS members.

However, he knew that his mother and his sisters would be interested in his assignment at a government-run children's mental hospital, named Aplerbach, in Dortmund. As the SS hospital representative of the Third Reich, he was responsible for making sure that directives from Berlin were carried out that certainly shortened the lifespan of the young patients at the hospital.

He jokingly described his job at Aplerbach as to not let any of the young patients escape while at the same time not letting any unauthorized visitors in. The reality was the visitors were usually distraught parents and grandparents who wanted to violate their once a month visitation privileges. He sugarcoated his explanation that the hardest part of his job was to greet grieving relatives arriving to pick up the gaunt remains of their deceased child. He told his family that many of the children patients, both Jewish and non-Jewish, were so deranged and heavily medicated that they did not eat and usually died of malnutrition. When his teary-eyed mother asked how often this happened, Ernst coldly replied, "At least two or three times a week. Even on weekends which interrupts my golf games."

To lighten his mother's worry about the strain on himself, which he personally didn't feel, Ernst told of his friendship with the on-call civilian medical doctor for the hospital, Dr. Eggert, and how they often ate dinner together and played golf every chance they could. Dr. Eggert wanted to become a surgeon, but he doubted that this would happen as the German graduate surgical training programs were now closed to Jewish doctors, including quarter-Jews like himself, under orders of the Minister of Health. Dr. Eggert was investigating ways to get out of Germany so he could pursue his life-long dream of becoming a surgeon. Like most Jews in Germany, he had heard of the free land offer in the Dominican Republic for Jews emigrating from Germany to escape the increasing wave of anti-semitism. But the practical reality was that Jews still had to get out of Germany and into a neutral country like Spain or Switzerland to start the journey to the Dominican Republic. Even though quarter-Jews like himself and Ernst had freedom to move about Germany and its conquered countries, they still had to make a border crossing and be accepted into a welcoming country to start the arduous odyssey to the Dominican Republic.

. . . .

On what was to be his final visit home to Berlin, Ernst was especially excited to tell his family, including his brother, Reinhard, home for a rare visit from his Warsaw SS assignment, about his promotion and new assignment to the eternal city of Rome where one of his main jobs would be to monitor the independent country of the Vatican. There were rumors that the Vatican was serving as a conduit for escaped criminals and prisoners of war, so it was going to be one of his responsibilities to shut down a Vatican based Roman Escape Line without angering the Pope and the millions of Catholics worldwide.

While Ernst and Reinhard were happy to be home, the brothers were anxious to have time together to talk about their new lives. They were able to get out the house under the guise of meeting friends at a local bierstube that just happened to have their family's stout beer on tap. They found a quiet corner table where Reinhard immediately expressed his concern for what was happening to his older brother, unfortunately caught up in the worst of the SS nefarious activities. Reinhard had tears in his eyes as he told Ernst that stories of the forced starvation and random killings of the children at the Dortmund Hospital were common knowledge throughout the SS in Germany and even had reached him at his SS assignment in Warsaw.

Ernst was seething inside that his younger brother would ruin this rare reunion by bringing up the unpleasantries of his hospital assignment. To deflect the spotlight from himself, Ernst reminded his brother that he could have been the one assigned to the hospital instead of his easy assignments of census taker, followed by supervising old Jewish engravers and printers that were forced to counterfeit money in a prison work camp, and now his current assignment of trying to apprehend a woman working in a Warsaw welfare office.

Reinhard's question, "Did you really have to kill those kids?" caused Ernst to bang his fist on the table, bouncing a head of beer out of their full steins.

Ernst finally replied in a quiet tone. "We were ordered to do it. Only the kids that weren't dying fast enough of starvation were injected with poison. Although, as the war went on, I seemed to be dealing with more and more Jewish parents coming to pick up their kids' bodies. All these kids were very sick in the head; otherwise they wouldn't have been there."

Reinhard took the beer-dampened napkin from under his stein to dry the tears from his eyes. He reached across the table to grasp his brother's stein-chilled hands. "After the war they will be looking to punish you and everyone else at that hospital for what happened to those helpless kids. You know that, don't you?'

"Germany can still win the war, so nothing will happen to me."

"Oh, Ernst! Dad's letters from the front lines say differently. Besides, would you really want that to happen?"

Like a good Nazi, Ernst's head nodded yes while Reinhard's shook no. They smiled sadly at each other realizing that they had to find a brotherly solution to this dilemma before Reinhard headed back to Warsaw and Ernst to his new assignment in Rome.

Reinhard's SS previous postings and current duties in Warsaw placed him geographically and politically more in the mainstream of the German war machine than Ernst's rather isolated assignment at the children's hospital in rural Germany. Reinhard's question of, "What do you know about your new boss in Rome, Colonel Kettler?" brought an indifferent shrug of Ernst's shoulders.

Ernst did make the observation that to rise to the rank of Colonel and be in charge of the German war effort in an important city like Rome indicated that he must be well-connected to the powers in Berlin, but also that he must be competent. Reinhard quietly added the words, 'and ruthless' to his brother thoughts.

One good thing that Reinhard had heard about Kettler was that Rome was falling behind in reaching its monthly quota of Jews being deported to the concentration camps and that the establishment of a Jewish ghetto in Rome, like the successful one in Warsaw, was taking longer than Berlin expected. Reinhard was hopeful that maybe this retarded progress was because Kettler was morally conflicted on the Jewish question. However, Kettler was blaming these issues on his lack of manpower to do these labor-intensive moves of the growingly recalcitrant Jews to the newly established ghetto or to the concentration camps. Ernst reassured his brother that his assignment involved detecting, monitoring, and then destroying the rumored Roman Escape Line. His job should not involve any persecution of his fellow Jews unless they were discovered as part of this Roman Escape Line.

Reinhard wanted to end their bierstube brotherly bonding on a happy note, so he asked his brother about his trip to the Dominican Republic with their Swiss bankers.

Ernst smiled and chuckled like the weight of the world was lifted from his shoulders. He mentioned that Trujillo gave all them a standing invitation to return to the Dominican Republic as his guests. This of course was before the war consumed Europe, but Ernst assumed that Trujillo's money was still hidden in his Swiss bank accounts. As a matter of fact, Ernst knew that Trujillo made good on his promise to provide free land to any Jewish refugees. A case in point was an old rabbi, named Heimo, from a town near Ernst's hospital assignment in Dortmund who had emigrated to the Dominican Republic to establish this Jewish settlement.

Rabbi Heimo's synagogue and home had been destroyed in the Kristallnacht violence, and his family was beaten and held hostage in the local jail until they promised to leave town. After nearly a week in jail, they were released and left town with their only possessions, the clothes that they were wearing.

Before the final swig of their family's stout, the brothers clinked their heavy steins in a toast that someday they would take a holiday in the welcoming Dominican Republic. This prophetic toast ultimately would have a profound effect on their lives.

III

Tom Gleason leaned over his fiancée Cindy to catch a glimpse of the spectacular Dominican Republic coast-line as their jet began its slow descent into Puerto Plata. The pilot earlier had pointed out the unmistakable border between Haiti and the Dominican Republic. The Haitian side, dark brown from having been stripped of its vegetation, looked like one big mudslide: past, present and future. In contrast the rolling Dominican side was verdant with cultivated fields of sugar cane as far as they could see from the descending jet that was delivering them for their wedding at the luxurious Iberostar resort later in the week. They were flying over undistinguishable resort towns and villages that had revitalized this Northern coast of the Dominican Republic since the decline of the sugar cane trade. Cindy had done her homework on the local area so that she could be a good host to the wedding party when they arrived. Pointing out of the jet's window for Tom to also see a larger coastal town, Cindy wondered if that could be Sosua. The Dominican Republic's Dictator Rafael Trujillo had given Sosua and adjoining acreage near their town of Puerto Plata, to Jewish refugees during the Second World War as a place for them to settle to escape Hitler's ruthless genocide. Cindy had a group visit of the wedding party to Sosua on her to-do list, if there was time after the wedding. They were getting a beautiful aerial view of the glistening silver water that sparked the Spanish explorers to name this tropical paradise, Puerto Plata, the Silver Port, as their plane, delivering them for their wedding at the Iberostar resort, made its final approach.

Tom and Cindy arrived before the rest of their guests to make sure that all the arrangements were in place for their marriage, which Tom lamely joked should be just a KISS. Cindy, getting the first and last word about the male-shunned preparations, agreed as long as he remembered that KISS meant: Keep It Short, Stupid. In spite of his steely, business-like Secret Service appearance, Tom was the romantic of the two and Cindy did not want to be caught off guard by one of his surprise romantic pranks, so she daily reinforced the KISS principle with him while exercising autocratic control over all facets of the wedding.

The only thing not under her all-pervasive purview was the bachelor party that Tom was quietly planning after the rest of the wedding party arrived. It took all of Cindy's restraint not to ask Tom what was planned for his first and last fling on the island.

Tom's comment, "You'd be surprised what we're doing," only heightened her anxiety about what she didn't know or have control over. Tom brought his golf clubs and went through the pretense of making tee times at the Jack Tar golf course adjacent to their Iberostar resort to focus Cindy's attention on this harmless golf outing that she couldn't object to. However, Tom threw a little gasoline on the fire by asking Cindy whether they should take male or the bikini-clad female caddies for the boys' round of golf. Her comment that his game was already bad enough without any female distraction was uttered without cracking a smile so he realized that she was operating with a very short fuse and he'd better not push his luck with his demonic Irish charm.

Cindy took that demonic Irish charm into consideration and had held the line on agreeing to their marriage until she was sure that Tom was a changed person from the person she met three years ago. Tom, to reinforce his less work-obsessed, newly changed person, had insisted that they go through a formal six-month pre-cana program like every other engaged couple in the Catholic Church was required to attend. Tom so badly wanted to win Cindy that he even went to the couple's pre-cana weekend retreat without the slightest protest. Cindy stalled off the wedding plans as long as she could, trying to assess if Tom was truly changed or just jumping through the hoops to get her to the altar, or in this case a flower-covered beach-side table under a colorful canopy. She needed time to decipher what was real and permanent in their relationship. She finally acquiesced as she gradually determined that Tom was now really different than the man she first met three years ago.

By Cindy and Tom's choice, their intimate destination wedding in the tropical paradise of the Dominican Republic was to be witnessed only by their wedding attendants. They were making plans for the obligatory back-home reception for family and friends a few weeks later—that is, "if we are still married," Cindy teased.

Like most couples doing the destination wedding phenomenon, they rolled their honeymoon into the same all-inclusive love-fest. This new-wave destination wedding generation willingly surrendered the intimate romantic honeymoon in a cozy little cabin in the Poconos or the Catskills for the more-or-less group honeymoon with their wedding party at their all-inclusive Dominican resort. In the early wedding planning stages, Tom, tongue-in-cheek, commented to Cindy that everything goes down-hill after the honeymoon, so they might as well start on the high ground with a Dominican Republic honeymoon.

IV

A battered red Chevrolet Impala cab, spewing a cloud of acrid smoke under the white-washed porte-cochere of the luxurious Iberostar resort, was waiting to take Tom, his best man, Neil and the groomsman David to their bachelor party in the nearby town of Puerto Plata. Fortunately, the wedding party's early morning flight from Washington, D.C. arrived on time thus allowing for the day-before-the-wedding activities, like the bachelor party, to proceed as scheduled.

Two or three blocks from the waterfront every Caribbean town is a carbon copy of another and the most prosperous islands look just like the least prosperous. It is just a matter of how far from the beach or main tourist areas that the poverty begins. Tom had promised his best man and groomsman that they were going to do something wild and illegal for their bachelor party the day before the wedding. To heighten their curiosity Tom, riding shot-gun in the rickety cab, turned to face his henchmen and asked them for one guess on what they were going to do for this one last fling. His best man, Neil, had tried to trick Cindy into telling him what the bachelor party plans were, but she pleaded total ignorance because of Tom's steely subterfuge about the bachelor outing. His groomsman David, a lifelong friend from their grade school days, in a bit of wishful thinking, threw out the notion that they could be headed for the biggest brothel in the Caribbean for a night of wild abandon.

David, ever-the-lawyer, asked Tom to clarify illegal. Brothels weren't illegal everywhere, case-in-point—Nevada, so they couldn't be headed for a brothel visit. Or could they? David wanted to retract his brothel suggestion, not so much because of his own illegality challenge, but because he knew that Tom would never put his married buddies or himself in such a compromised position the night before his wedding. By the time David could venture another guess, or Neil even get out his first guess, Tom was peeling off a few pesos from his money clip to pay the cab driver who was holding up three fingers, indicating the fare as effectively as any dash-mounted metering machine. The hotel bellman had given the cabbie their destination in Spanish and how much the fare would be to avoid the overcharging hassle that often found gringo tourists in a threatening situation in an unsavory section of town.

The three macho tourists, colorfully dressed for their big outing, felt strength in their numbers as the smoking cab dropped them off two blocks from their destination on a narrow street littered with smashed toys, flat-tired bicycles and abandoned cars. The cabbie pointed ahead and told them to follow all the men who were escaping the post-siesta tedium of hanging out in their sweltering shacks with no jobs and wives gone to work as domestics in the resort hotels. Negotiating the obstacle course behind a few plainly dressed natives, they could feel the tension building like they were walking into the exercise compound of a maximum security Federal Prison.

Tom tried not to display his apprehension, but he was betrayed by his darting, Secret Service eyes panning the locals on both sides of the street. These locals were intrigued by the three out-of-place gringos trudging up the street. Tom felt some small measure of relief with the realization that these mostly unemployed denizens could not afford guns to rob them if they were so inclined. However, a razor-sharp knife used to bone a scrawny chicken on their front stoop or a sugarcane machete was another story, even though he had been assured that this was a safe area during daylight hours as long as they stayed together. Around a corner Tom could see their destination, the only two-story building towering over the neighboring plywood and tar-paper shacks.

The English-speaking hotel concierge, Carlos, had promised that he would meet them at the entrance gate to the gallera to explain the wild action inside as everything happened in Spanish. Carlos immediately recognized the three gringos and briskly approached, giving them a firm hand shake with the obligatory, "Buenos Dias."

Tom's and his two buddies nodded their heads and replied, "Good afternoon, Carlos."

Carlos explained that general admission to the cockfighting stadium was in standing-room-only on the upper tier and cost 1 peso.

Reserved seats in the five rows below the standing-room-only balcony were 3 pesos. These multi-colored fiberglass seats, cracked and chipped bowling alley rejects, started at the dirt level fighting pit. The highly coveted first row seats put occupants' feet on the same bloody dirt floor where the two cocks fought and their handlers sat.

The elevated standing-room-only area was separated from the reserved seating below by a bent and rusty floor-to-ceiling cyclone fence that effectively kept the two areas and their different clientele separated except for an occasional beer that would be thrown down at the cocks in the fighting pit by the rowdy patrons expressing their displeasure at their losing cock. The two pesos extra for reserved seating was an effective segregator, keeping the haves and have-nots in their respective places so that everyone could bet and enjoy the fights with their peers.

Since Tom was hosting this bachelor party he handed Carlos twenty-pesos and held up four fingers, indicating to Carlos to buy four reserved tickets because they needed him to sit with them to explain the subtleties of betting on the high-strung roosters. The husky, halter-topped cashier, who was her own security guard, was seated on a tilting three-legged stool behind a shoebox that served as the cash box. She scribbled four seat numbers on a piece of scrap paper and slide it to Carlos under the rusty chicken wire that separated her from the customers eager to get inside for the gruesome action of the afternoon cockfights.

. . . .

Once inside the cockfight grounds, Tom assessed the dreary surroundings and could sense the curious fleeting glances of the other patrons as the three of them were the only gringos within the graffiti stained stucco walls of this poor working- man's retreat. Before going to their seats in the fighting arena, Carlos led them to the noisy walled-off back corner where older men were seated at a deeply clawed bench. They were wrestling with a struggling cock that had a thick black rubber band made from an old bicycle inner tube tire around its beak to keep it from pecking out the eyes of these seasoned handlers.

Younger men with bloody scratches and bumpy keloidal scars on their forearms from training these high-strung roosters were helping to restrain the nervous cocks as the older men were taping razor-sharp plastic spurs over the little stump that remained after the roosters' dewclaws were removed shortly after birth. These roosters were bred to fight to the death and the little convex dewclaw bump served as a stabilizing point for the concave mini cup of the lethal spur. The roosters' owners, standing on their tip-toes to observe this critical appendage application, rely on these experienced tapers and their assistants to get the proper angle on the spur so that a quick flick of the rooster's foot can mean instant death to the other rooster in the ring.

Tom's apprehensive yet curious party kept their distance even as Carlos tried to draw them closer to observe the talent of the old men applying these lethal spurs. They did lean in, trying to better understand the very animated discussion between a shouting old-man taper and an obviously distraught owner demanding that one of the plastic spurs be re-taped at a different angle to provide for a more efficient one-stroke kill. Observing these two vociferous combatants, Tom wondered how the actual cockfight could be any more intense than this taping of the lethal spur controversy was.

Carlos explained that the taping-on of these lethal spurs was like flipping a switch, activating these highly trained roosters into a lethal killing machine. Either a white—blanco—or a black—negro—ankle band was attached to each rooster. In each of tonight's ten-match schedule a white-banded cock would fight a black-banded opponent.

. . . .

The well-endowed ticket taker with the too-small green halter top now walked around the crowded compound ringing a dented old cow bell as a signal for all to proceed to their seats in the cock-fighting gallera. On their way to their seats, they paused briefly at the taping tables where the roosters were being prepared in the order of their appearance on the fight card. After the spurs were inspected and approved by the cock's owner, they were put in a burlap sack and weighed on a primitive type of produce scale to the nearest half of a pound because the cocks must fight another cock that weighs within one-half pound of its opponent.

It was obvious that Carlos was a regular at the cockfights as everyone greeted him as he escorted the three gringos to their third row seats across from the entrance ramp. When two of the largest uniformed humans that Tom had ever seen walked slowly down the ramp, the boisterous crowd started to quiet. "Private police," Carlos whispered to Tom, who nodded his agreement as his Secret Service training again kicked in. Tom observed these two men quickly scanning the boisterous gallera, obviously as advance men for an important person about to enter the stadium. Their gaze momentarily locked on Tom and his two companions, probably because they were the only gringos in the stadium and they were a bit overdressed in their khakis and brightly colored polo shirts compared to the locals in faded tee shirts and worn blue jeans.

Out of the corner of his eye Tom saw Carlos give the private police a discrete thumbs-up indicating that everything was cool with the three gringo interlopers. Tom was not sure how much legal authority these two burly private guards had and he certainly didn't plan on finding out as they could make short order of his wimpy wedding party. Tom followed Carlos' lead by standing up when the ticket-taker lady came down the short ramp to the dirt floor, carrying a boom box that was blaring out the Dominican National Anthem. She was followed down the ramp by two officially dressed policemen escorting a portly, well-dressed man. When the scratchy nation anthem concluded, this VIP, like arriving royalty, did a slow 360-degree turn waving to the boisterous crowd. Tom got Carlos' attention with a shrug of his shoulders and a head feint toward the obviously important occupant of the front row across from them. Carlos whispered the name, Ludwig, to Tom which brought another shrug of the shoulders from Tom.

· · · ·

The spectators grew quiet when two handlers, one wearing a white wristband and the other a black wristband, walked down the ramp to the dirt floor of the circular fighting pit. They each carried a burlap bag cinched closed by a short length of rope with a loop that was put over a hook on opposite sides of an old fashion scale. Once the bagged cocks settled down while suspended from each end of the scale used to determine that they were of similar weight, the anxious crowd started chanting "blanco" or "negro" depending on their favored bird.

The handlers held up their un-bagged roosters as they circled the ten-foot fighting pit. As interesting as Tom found the fight preparations in the pit, the real action was in the stands as people were starting to bet a few pesos with each other. He had been expecting to step up to a betting window as in horse racing. Carlos had tried to prepare the gringos for the intensity of the betting action. The action started with picking a rooster, either blanco or negro, and then making eye contact with anyone in the seats around you who might be waving his hand while shouting his preferred color choice, different than yours.

The spectators in the standing room only section that ringed the five rows of seats below them were the most animated as they stamped their feet and yanked on the cyclone fence that kept them separated from the seated spectators below. Once eye contact was made with someone shouting the opposite color of what you were shouting, you held up fingers to indicate how many pesos you wanted to bet with your opponent. Carlos had warned them not to bet with the upper-tier spectators as it was easy for them to disappear into the back row or down the exit ramp if they lost their bet with you. You literally would be taking your life in your own hands if you went upstairs to try to collect your winnings.

Carlos had also warned them not to bet more than a few pesos as this is a lot of money, probably a day's wages for most local bettors while to a vacationing gringo it was the cost of a beer.

Carlos's final advice was not to bet more than ten-pesos with Ludwig, seated across from them, as he took great pleasure in beating naïve gringos because of his knowledge of the fighting lineage of the roosters in any given match. The cockfights were much too low an overhead operation to print programs like the horse racing forums, so there was no written record of a rooster's lineage and fighting record. The breeding of fighting cocks, like racehorses, often determined the winning rooster regardless of their training and fighting history.

Tom gave Carlos three pesos to bet for them with the apology that they were too chicken to bet for themselves and they would watch him in this first match to see how it was done. Carlos told them to observe the roosters for any telltale signs of post weigh-in cowering or intimidation after they were un-bagged. He commented to his three students that he always picked the rooster that was the most nervous and agitated, hoping that this energy would carry over into a lethal aggression that would quickly overwhelm the other rooster.

Carlos only had to shout "blanco" once when his darting eye made contact with Ludwig's steely gaze as he shouted back "negro," while holding up his hand with all five digits extended.

Tom immediately thought of Carlos' warning to never bet more than ten-pesos with him because he knew the blood-lines of all the roosters. Tom was getting two more pesos from his money clip to give to Carlos to match Ludwig's five peso offer when Carlos held up three fingers to counter Ludwig's opening bet of five-pesos on negro. Ludwig, nodding his head, held up three fingers and Carlos did the same to seal the bet at three pesos. Tom offered Carlos two more pesos to make another bet, but Carlos waved off this extra money with the comment, "One bet's enough for the first match."

The clamor and noise of the first match betting was quieting down when the referee went to the center of the fighting pit and surveyed the restless crowd. Tom noticed the referee make quick eye contact with Ludwig who gave a nod of his head followed by a short blast of the referee's Bobbie style whistle hanging from a blood-stained lanyard around his neck.

The two handlers lowered their squirming roosters to the dirt floor of the fighting pit and retreated to two folding chairs on opposite sides of the dirt pit where they had to stay seated until the match was over and the referee signaled for them to attend to their rooster, dead or alive. A large timer clock mounted over the entry ramp set to five minutes was started.

Tom found himself, like everyone in the small circular arena, sliding to the front of his seat and leaning forward as far as he could toward the roosters while shouting, "Blanco, go blanco," at the prancing and preening combatants. Except for Ludwig, all the seated spectators assumed this same animated posture and the standing room crowd above them stomped their feet and jerked on the enclosing cyclone fencing. Ludwig sat back in his seat with his arms confidently folded across his large barrel chest. Dispassionately, he stared straight ahead as his eyes were shooting laser beams at the blanco rooster trying to take his negro rooster out of the match. Tom wondered how long it took Ludwig to grow so dispassionate at the violence being waged in front of him.

The handlers defied gravity as their folding chairs tipped and teetered on their front legs as the horizontal handlers were screaming encouragement into the ears of their respective rooster. The obnoxious cacophony of the crowd screaming their blancos and negros brought Tom to his senses as he realized that the roosters did not know the color of the band on their scrawny ankles so why scream at them? The speed of their pecking heads amazed Tom and once the cocks got close to each other they would jump and make a swiping pass with their newly taped lethal appendage, hoping to lacerate or puncture the flopping wattle of their evasive opponent.

As the clock was ticking down below two minutes, it was obvious that the roosters were tiring as their pecking moves slowed and the lunging jumps stopped. The negro bird appeared the most exhausted as it just pivoted in one spot while the blanco rooster slowly circled, closing in for the kill. Finally, the totally exhausted negro bird tired of defending itself sat down and then collapsed on its side, all the time being pecked to death by the winning blanco bird. With just 30 seconds left on the clock, the referee hovering over the one sided action glanced toward the impassive Ludwig who was shaking his head no. The fight must go on to the end.

Mercifully a buzzer sounded when the time clock reached zero and the referee grasped the blanco bird by its neck and passed it to its handler. The negro handler picked up his unresponsive bird, probably tonight's dinner, and stuffed it in the gunnysack and headed up the ramp. The blanco bird did the obligatory short victory lap in the outstretched arms of its proud, grinning handler. Half the audience was smiling, receiving their winning bets from the losing side. Tom noticed a slight grin crack Ludwig's stoic face as he handed three pesos to the jubilant Carlos, who was jumping up and down as if he had just won a million dollar lottery. Tom thought it strange for Ludwig to smile when he lost ,and Tom couldn't help but notice the dark scar on the underside of Ludwig's left upper arm as he extended it to pass the three pesos to Carlos.

V

Cindy and her wedding attendants were relieved when the men left the resort for their bachelor party. Now they could get down to the necessary girl things for tomorrow's wedding. One supposed advantage of a destination wedding is that everything is taken care of by the resort, thus freeing the wedding party to enjoy their beautiful tropical setting. Yesterday, Tom and Cindy checked on the resort's list of responsibilities and everything that they had contracted for was organized and ready to go.

Today, Cindy wanted her bridal party to try on their outfits to be sure that everyone had everything that they needed with no last minutes panic shopping trips, as there were no bridal salons in Puerto Plata. After the giggles and laughter of the three women, wiggling and pushing each other into tomorrow's clothes, subsided, Cindy announced, "Let's go shopping, and you have to wear your bathing suits." The women all laughed, knowing about the non-existent shopping around the resort, but nevertheless they agreed to meet in fifteen minutes at the pool to begin their bachelorette shopping party.

Cindy was wearing a broad brimmed straw hat to protect her face from the searing tropical sun because of tomorrow's pictures. Only Joanne, the maid of honor, had the physique and the courage to wear a skimpy bikini when the ladies met at the Iberostar's free-formed meandering pool that would have stretched out to be as long as a football field if straightened out. "We're gong to the Orange Mall," Cindy announced like a true girl-scout leader to the questioning look of Joanne and Mary. They each tucked their pesos into areas of their swimming suits that only they dared to venture.

At the sparkling beach, Cindy pointed to her right toward a distant faded orange building that almost could be a mirage caused by the brilliant sun reflecting off the sand and scrub foliage on either side of a little river emptying into the ocean.

About half-way to this intriguing orange building, Joanne, the obviously athletic maid of honor, commented that she felt funny wearing her bikini. The other ladies, looking down at their own modest one-piece suits, poorly disguising their prematurely sagging physiques, reassured her that she looked fantastic and that she was the only one of them who could get away with wearing such a revealing suit.

"No, that's not the problem," she said. "I feel funny walking past all these flabby women sunning on the beach who are only wearing a monokini. If they can get away with it, so can I." She no sooner finished saying this than her hand undid the little clasp holding her top on. Cindy nonchalantly mentioned that she might need to put her top back on when they got to the mall to avoid a traffic jam from male gawkers.

The three of them splashed in and out of the shallow water at the edge of the beach to avoid the scorching sand on their feet as they headed toward the euphemistically named Orange Mall. Approaching the mall they walked past a large estate that had a guard seated on a bench at the top of the low barrier dune. He was armed with a camera with a long telephoto lens pointed at them. Before Joanne could put her top back on the camera-man smiled and lowered his camera, obviously having already taken pictures of the embarrassed, topless Joanne.

The girls thought for a minute about confronting him, but

had second thoughts when they saw the rifle across his legs and another security guard on the deck of the ocean-front mansion behind him. "So much for having a little fun," Joanne commented as she too-late became a bikini lady again.

The old Quonset hut that had been sprayed painted orange to make it visible for miles up and down the beach was partitioned into booths and stalls that allowed the local crafters and artisans to display their wares. Cindy called a huddle with Joanne and Mary before they entered the mall. She extracted her money from one of those feminine hiding spots and gave Joanne and Mary each 50 pesos to buy their bridesmaid's gift. Ever the practical one, Cindy explained that she didn't have room to carry any gifts from home and this way they could each get a local gift as a remembrance of the wedding weekend. The girls had a group hug before beginning their shopping. Cindy decided that she had better keep an eye on Joanne to keep her from getting backed into a corner by a Caribbean lover boy who viewed her skimpy bikini as an invitation for a little fun.

The girls perused the local handicrafts that had a distinctive Dominican flavor. The hand decorated wicker baskets, purses and hats provided many a laugh as they modeled them with brightly colored muumuus and scarves. Of course the exquisite hand-made jewelry made their splurge decisions even more difficult.

They were thinking of finishing their shopping, when an unshaven, uniformed man with a camera hanging from a broad neck-strap, approached Joanne. "You come with me," he ordered in halting English.

She crossed her arms across her chest, trying for a degree of modesty as the man's dark eyes avoided eye contact and bore into her chest. "Why?" was her only response.

"Have pictures of you naked, walking on my private beach," he said as he took the camera off his neck as if handing it to her.

"So? Many other women were not wearing tops," she replied while turning away to find the other girls.

He put his hand on her bare shoulder, trying to turn her around to face him, which he didn't have to do as she freely spun around and buried her knee in his groin. He doubled up in agony, falling to his knees as his camera went bouncing on the sandy concrete, "Bitch, you pay Bitch."

The other girls heard the commotion and came to Joanne's side as a circle of curious tourists and stall-keepers formed around them. Joanne picked up the camera that landed at her feet. The camera back had sprung open when it bounced on the concrete, exposing the roll of film to the bright afternoon sun rendering it useless. Another uniformed guard appeared out of the crowd and bent over his still moaning colleague. Cindy grabbed a tie-dyed tee shirt from the nearest booth for Joanne to slip on to lessen the distraction caused by her skimpy bikini. Joanne's practiced eye immediately noticed that the uniforms of the two cops were different. The fallen officer's seemed to be of the rent-a-cop variety, while the other seemed to be an official police uniform with a badge, handcuffs and a pistol hanging from a large belt that was already strained to hold the protuberant belly above it.

"Let's get back to the hotel," Cindy whispered to the girls. "We can finish shopping later." She tossed 10 pesos to the lady behind the tee shirt booth. "Keep the change."

"Stay," the real officer barked as he saw the girls trying to back out of the every growing circle. "Why did you assault this officer? You can be arrested."

"He assaulted me. Nobody touches me without my permission. Nobody!" Joanne screamed as she half-threw him the camera with the now useless film. The entire circle started to back up anticipating further confrontation while the girls formed their own tighter huddle.

The injured cop slowly rose to his feet, still painfully bending over trying to avoid grabbing his throbbing crotch. Joanne had difficulty suppressing a smile as her CIA training achieved its desired effect. A well-dressed, distinguished man wearing a name tag indicating that he was the mall manager rushed over to the two officers and after a brief conference announced, "All okay.

Please, everybody, go back to shopping."

The crowd slowly dispersed and the mall manager approached the girls who felt in a state of limbo with the two cops still glaring at them. Joanne was relieved to see that the injured rent-a-cop was not armed and that the film in the camera was now useless as evidence. "Who does he work for?" Joanne asked the mall manager.

"He's the guard for a very important person who owns the big house where no nude bathing is permitted on his private beach. Our European vacationers are the ones who usually get in trouble on his private beach, as it is their custom to go topless. You are the first Americans to violate the law on his property. You will have to talk to the police when they come to your hotel to possibly arrest you. This is the way the police handle these cases."

Joanne had all she could do to restrain herself from drop kicking the mall manager as the real cop approached them. Looking at the girls' blue Iberostar wrist-bands he said, "I will meet you in the Iberostar lobby tomorrow night at 6 pm to plead guilty and pay your fine of 50 pesos and 50 pesos for my expenses."

Cindy moved in front of the still fuming and about to erupt Joanne to prevent her from taking on the real cop, which would have landed all of them in a dreaded Caribbean jail. "Sorry, she can't meet you tomorrow. She is the maid-of- honor at my wedding tomorrow afternoon. How about the next day?"

The rent-a-cop, now standing a little more erect, overheard Cindy's offer of postponed justice and interjected, "Mr. Walther isn't going to like this delay. His camera has been ruined by this American bitch. She must pay!"

Cindy shuffled sideways a couple steps to stay between Joanne and the reenergized rent-a-cop. She slipped her prescription Reva sunglasses off and looked straight in the faces of both cops. "Look at me. Don't you know who I am? I don't think you want to mess with us too much longer."

The realization that this incident may be getting a little beyond his pay grade brought out the cop's conciliatory offer. "We can settle this case here and now for 200 pesos and this case disappears."

Cindy reached into her swimsuit top and retrieved her stash of slightly sweaty and sandy folded bills. "Looks like I am a little short."

As she was starting to hand the money to the over-eager cop, who probably would have settled for any amount of money, Mary the unobtrusive third member of the beleaguered trio, pushed Cindy's outstretched arm back to her side. "No. Don't give it to them. This is a scam, an illegal shakedown. I'll fight it in court. They have no evidence because the film is ruined." Mary took one step toward the two cops. "Come to the hotel with your legal paperwork and we'll settle the case then." The girls quickly turned and headed to the beach for the hike back to their hotel.

They walked with a quickened pace, with one eye over their shoulders. Joanne kept tugging down on her festive tie-dyed shirt so that it was starting to be long enough for a sleeping shirt by the time they were passing the scene of the crime. The beach front voyeur with the smashed camera was probably in the house icing his privates to keep down the swelling from Joanne's well placed knee, but they could see his cohort still on the mansion's expansive deck with a pair of binoculars and a camera zeroed in on them. "Should we tell the men about our little adventure?" Cindy threw out, not knowing what answer to expect from the other girls?

"I can't wait to tell Neil. He'll be so proud of me executing the disabling knee thrust just like he trained me in our CIA self-defense class. This was the first time I've done it to anyone not having extra padding in the crotch. Wow, it really works!"

"I agree we have to tell them, but let's wait until after the wedding tomorrow so that we don't take away from your day," Mary offered.

"Don't worry about me, Mary. The wedding will go off as planned," Cindy said.

"That may be true," Mary agreed, "but let's just wait until after the wedding. We told these jokers not to come tomorrow. They probably won't show up at all."

The three of them nodded their heads in agreement to this post-wedding confession, when they would all be together to share this unbelievable story of making a mountain out of a molehill.

VI

The three gringos gradually grew more confident increasing their betting frequency and amount wagered in subsequent rounds of the cockfights, even occasionally going against the obviously well-healed Ludwig in small wagers below their self imposed limit of ten-pesos. Carlos kept a watchful eye on every bet that the trio made as the losing party often developed selective amnesia unless eye contact was reestablished and an open palm extended to collect their winnings after each fight.

After the fourth fight Carlos asked them not to make more than two wagers apiece since he could only keep track of six bets with their ever-allusive betting opponents. Between fights the well-endowed ticket lady carried a stainless steel pail, dripping with condensation, as a roving concession stand selling cold green bottles of locally brewed Presidente beer. Tom had been to enough sporting events, where beer was free flowing, to know that as the fight card progressed the action would intensify and a well-functioning brain would be imperative to avoid being taken to the cleaners by the more sober natives who couldn't afford to buy as many beers as the rich gringos.

Tom noticed that Ludwig always had a definite color preference for each fight and that his choice seemed to win more than it lost.

Ludwig sat back in his chair and watched each fight with a quiet detachment in marked contrast to everyone else in the gallera who would stand and shout their crude encouragement to their chosen rooster. Tom could not help but notice another small dark tattoo on Ludwig's left forearm as he extended his hand to square-up his bets after each fight. Tom asked Neil to check it out, but Neil mentioned that he had noticed it earlier and thought it was a smudge of dirt. Tom smiled at this suggestion as the meticulously dressed Ludwig wouldn't be caught dead with dirty forearms and besides the area was almost a perfect rectangle as no dirt mark would be.

After the fifth fight, Tom welcomed the half-way-point intermission. The fifth fight had been particularly bloody and gruesome and Tom's ears were ringing from the auditory overload of the patrons screaming their encouragements to the listless and supine blanco rooster as well as to the predatory negro cock. Tom had to turn his head to avoid looking at the negro cock pecking away at the eyes of the fallen blanco cock and he wondered why the fight wasn't stopped early by the referee. Out of the corner of his eye he noticed Ludwig wearing a strange sardonic smile as the macabre scene continued to play out on the dirt ring at his feet. Finally, he nodded his head and gave a hand signal to the referee to stop the fight as the unmoving blanco cock was now blind and dead. As Ludwig paid off his losing wagers on his fallen blanco cock, Tom thought it strange that he had a perverse look on his face that said, 'Even though I lost my bets, wasn't that fun?'

Ludwig's two bodyguards quickly led the way up the ramp and the rest of the crowd followed as the air in the arena was getting a little close with all the animated hot bodies pressing against each other in their betting frenzies. Tom found the interactions in the gallera more interesting than the cocks fighting in the pit and he viewed the betting as a vehicle to interact with the locals and to share in their unique customs. Many of the men hurried to the pee corner before it became a raging river, opting to skip the overflowing one-hole toilet that was the grossest thing the trio had ever seen or smelt.

Ludwig was observed nursing a Presidente sitting in a dark corner of the make-shift bar behind the ticket booth. Three men went in to see him for short visits and, to a man, they exited with relieved smiles on their faces. Tom commented to Carlos that this whole scene was like the king holding court with his subjects meekly approaching to gain the king's favor. Carlos commented that this was the usual protocol and it seemed to be the reason for the intermission. Carlos speculated that many of the supplicants were seeking favors, or possibly a job from Ludwig since he was general manager of the local Brugal rum distillery. The rumors around Puerto Plata had it that Ludwig came from a German family that owned breweries in Hitler's Germany. He arrived with the last group of Jewish immigrants from Spain near the end of WWII. The Dominican Republic was the only Western hemisphere country that accepted Jewish refuges from Germany or other countries of war-torn Europe. The German immigrants made a perceptible impact on this area of the Dominican Republic settling in their own ocean-side town of Sosua. Ludwig came to be one of the immigrants' biggest success stories resurrecting the Brugal rum distillery from its languishing post-war doldrums.

The trio joked among themselves about who was going to be the lucky one to prostrate himself before Ludwig in the dark corner of the bar to request betting tips for the second-half of the fight card. The second-half of the fight card could not begin until Ludwig returned to his seat. Fortunately, Ludwig emerged from his shadowy court and headed back into the gallera before they had solved their dilemma. Back in their seats Carlos asked how everyone was doing with their betting. Like any gambler not wanting to admit to his true losses, Tom mentioned that he was up a couple pesos and he should quit while he was ahead. Groomsman David, the ever- cautious lawyer, noncommittally shrugged his shoulders, and Neil pretended not to hear the question.

Tom wondered about the deferential treatment that Ludwig received, even by the supposedly impartial referee, as they waited for him to give the signal to start the sixth fight. Tom had been holding up two fingers while shouting blanco and Ludwig immediately countered with three fingers, voicing negro. Tom made the instantaneous acceptance to Ludwig by holding up three fingers for his blanco rooster. The sixth round was the least violent of any of the previous rounds. The cocks seemed more interested in prancing and preening than in actual combat. Toward the end of the five-minute time limit Tom's blanco rooster started chasing and harmlessly peeking at the tail feathers shielding the oily, fragrant uropygial gland of the retreating negro opponent. The bettors on both sides screamed obscenities at the non-combative roosters trying to stimulate a confrontation.

The five-minute end-of-match bell sounded and the referee looked at Ludwig who busied himself with ordering a Presidente from the jack-of-all-trades waitress. The referee gave a quick blow of his whistle to end the non-fight of the two reluctant cocks. To resounding boos, the referee needlessly shouted, "Draw!" The gringos felt relieved that they had not lost any more pesos as no money changes hands in this rather rare draw outcome. Carlos leaned over and explained that the referee, usually after looking at the gallera owner Ludwig, can declare one of the roosters the victor if he was the clear aggressor, but in this match with no obvious aggressor, the referee did not want to risk a riot, especially in the upper deck standing crowd, so he declared the draw.

Lawyer David asked what happens to these two peace-loving roosters. "Can they ever fight again?"

Carlos gave the slash across the throat, "Dinner tonight."

The fight card proceeded uneventfully with the three gringos gradually becoming more self-reliant, but always under the watchful eye of Carlos until the tenth and final match of the day. Carlos quickly explained that during this final match, bets could be increased between bettors who had bets established before the match started. "Be careful," he cautioned. "You can lose more in this final match than all the other rounds combined." He explained that the biggest and strongest cocks are entered in this final match. There is no time limit so it is a fight to death or until one of the handlers belatedly tries to rescue his defenseless cock, thus conceding the match and incurring the wrath of all the loosing bettors.

Tom observed the frantic betting all around him and he noticed that a couple bettors, who seemed to win more than they lost in previous matches, were betting on the blanco rooster. Avoiding direct eye contact he could tell that Ludwig was trying to get bets against the negro rooster that he was betting on. Tom had to make a quick decision whether to challenge Ludwig, who seemed to have inside info on the stronger roosters or should he rely on the instincts of the winning bettors in the stands near him. A count down from ten to zero, when all opening bets had to be placed, was started. At ocho Tom found himself locked in eye contact with Ludwig who was thrusting both open hands toward him while mouthing negro. Tom's opening and closing fingers, like a minaret being manipulated by ten strings, confirmed his bet of ten-pesos on blanco. The spectators always seemed to be aware of what Ludwig was doing and the arena went quiet as Ludwig's big bet—most likely to grow larger—registered with everyone. Tom didn't see Carlos roll his eyes as if to say, 'you're in deep trouble.'

As the high-strung cocks were lowered to the dirt floor and released by their handlers, Tom thought, 'it's only money' and this was his last bachelor fling where he wouldn't have to account for ill-spent money to a questioning spouse as would be the case after tomorrow's wedding. Each cock made numerous valiant but futile jumps and slashes with the hooks taped to their dewclaw stubs. Tom felt groomsman David's hand grasp the back of his belt to restrain him from falling into the rows ahead or even into the fighting pit as he leaned forward to scream encouragement to his blanco cock.

Ludwig was sitting passively with crossed arms. Tom's hands opened and closed indicating his desire to double his bet to 20-pesos on blanco. Ludwig didn't want to appear overly eager to accept Tom's challenge so he went though the charade of leaning forward to observe the condition of his negro cock. There was no discerning any advantage to either cock from the action so far in the pit. As Ludwig watched Tom's eyes and hands frantically open and close two times raising the stakes to thirty-pesos. Ludwig pounced on Tom's overly eager raise from ten to thirty-pesos by opening and closing his hands twice.

Carlos thought that Tom had made a careless mistake and cautioned him that he was at thirty-pesos, which earned him a casual shrug of Tom's shoulder. The cocks inadvertently heightened the drama by quickly circling the pit with only an occasional peck at their opponent. Tom figured that the longer this fight went on, the better chance his blanco cock had as the negro cock was obviously the early favorite. Otherwise Ludwig wouldn't have picked it. After a few more minutes of the cock's chasing each other around in circles, Tom opened and closed his hands one more time to increase the bet to forty-pesos. Ludwig went through his stalling tactics again so as to not appear overly eager for the increase. However, after scanning the quieting spectators and the prancing cocks, he returned two hand pumps to increase the bet to fifty-pesos. Without hesitation Tom returned two hand pumps back to Ludwig confirming the bet at fifty-pesos.

Tom, from his earliest days of playing sports and now in his Secret Service career, always liked to see how his opponent operated under the pressure of the moment assuming that he could keep his own emotions under control. He was not sure that he had Ludwig to his breaking point. This would be determined as the cockfight played out. Tom felt certain that he had his own emotions under control.

However, Carlos sat back in his seat, pressing his sweaty palms against his temples, while mumbling that he had never seen fifty-pesos bet in all his years of going to cockfights. Fifty-pesos was more money than many Dominicans make in a month he thought. The spectators grew silent, almost neglecting the two cocks engaged in their lethal sparring match, as all eyes were on Ludwig and Tom.

Tom felt hundreds of eyes like lasers burning through him, but he never took his eyes off Ludwig, who was now twisting and turning in his old bowling alley seat with his eyes rapidly darting between the hushed gallera and the fighting cocks. Tom did not entertain the idea of increasing the bet as he saw what he had wanted to in his now nervous opponent, and he was equally sure that Ludwig would not raise the fifty-pesos bet which would only draw more unwanted attention to himself and the challenging gringo outsider.

Tom was so intent on watching every reaction of Ludwig, especially his deeply sunk, emotionless eyes that he missed the fatal jump and quick claw swipe that ended the highest betting round in recent memory at the gallera. The stands erupted with the screams of the losers and the joyous shouts of the winners. In the deafening clamor Tom couldn't discern which cock had won until a fifty-dollar bill was shoved in his lap by one of Ludwig's burly bodyguards. Tom looked in horror, but not in total surprise, as he watched Ludwig walk across the bloody dirt pit and kick his dead negro cock into the second row of seats. Tom grasped the fifty-dollar bill, giving little thought to the fact that it was more than their fifty-pesos bet that he had just won.

After the angry Ludwig departed, Tom accepted Carlos's belated congratulations for besting Ludwig. "I have never seen Ludwig so mad. It's not the money - he has a lot - he was embarrassed because no one ever stands up to him and wins like you did."

Tom took pleasure in not only winning the bet but in breaking the impenetrable façade of someone who thought himself invincible.

VII

Carlos insisted on escorting the three gringos out of the gallera and down the littered street to a main intersection where they could hail a cab back to the hotel. Everyone leaving the gallera knew that Tom had won many pesos, so Carlos felt compelled to watch their backsides, unaware of Tom's secret service training and best man Neil Gibson's CIA background. To the unsuspecting Dominicans they looked like the typical carefree American tourists who could be easily robbed on a deserted side street. Tom was feeling flush after besting Ludwig in the final high-stake cockfight, so he offered to buy a round of Presidente at an open air bar overlooking the protected silvery bay that Puerto Plata was named after and built around.

Fortunately Puerto Plata was not on the cruise ships' itineraries so the downtown area was still local shops and bars without the scourge of the multi-island chain jewelry stores that let tourists buy their jewelry on one island and then exchange it a day later on another island.

After they were seated at a table overlooking the silvery water of the ripple-less bay that was turning reddish-orange from the setting sun, they were approached by a boy toting a shoeshine box. Carlos tried to wave the boy off warning his friends that this would only be the start of a parade of street children trying to earn a few pesos. However, David and Neil welcomed the boy and had their leather loafers cleaned and polished. Tom pointed to his dusty white tennis shoes with a dismissive wave but the beaming young salesman was a step ahead, holding up a bottle of chalky white slurry to rehab Tom's sneakers. After his shoe whitewash Tom said that Ludwig was going to pay for the shoe shines so he gave the boy an exorbitant ten-pesos with the exhortation to give it to his parents. When the boy picked up his shoe shine box and turned to leave, the four of them smiled simultaneously as they noticed the latest Sony CD player hanging on the back of the shoe shine box. Tom's comment of, "He'll be able to buy all the latest pirated CD's after this stop," brought a round of laughter and a green bottle toast from the four amigos. After this eye-opener on the local economy, they didn't feel so guilty about not buying any of the pirated tapes, movies and tee shirts that were being peddled non-stop to them by the cutest, cleanest and probably richest children of Puerto Plata. They were nursing their Presidentes down to their last couple swigs and David wondered if they would have an afternoon free later in the week to return for another cockfight session. Tom was surprised to hear his conservative lawyer groomsman express this interest as he was the one doing the least wagering and was the most reserved during some of the crazier moments, especially Tom's final encounter with Ludwig.

Carlos mentioned that the cockfights are not staged every day, so he would check the schedule and let them know. David wondered if Ludwig came to every fight. Carlos went momentarily silent before replying that he usually does since he owns the gallera. Carlos mentioned that Ludwig is also into breeding and training the fighting cocks and has genetic doctors in Germany helping him develop the perfect breed of fighting cocks. Ludwig, trying to curry the favor of the other local breeders as he still considers himself an outsider, has supplied newly hatched chicks to his competitors in the hope that the gallera would stay open.

Tom brought a smile to the group's face when he offered to give

Ludwig his money back if he needed it to keep the gallera afloat. Carlos got an especially good laugh out of this before he informed the group that Ludwig was the richest person in Puerto Plata and lived in the biggest house on the beach, not too far from their hotel. As long as the local Brugal rum plant was struggling to keep up with all its orders, Ludwig would not have to worry about needing a loan to cover his cockfight losses. Carlos said that years ago Ludwig gave his brother, right off the plane from Spain, a job in the shipping department at the Brugal warehouse, where he has worked his way up to become the head of the shipping department. Carlos' brother tells him that many rum orders are shipped to Europe, especially Germany. However, enough rum stays in the Dominican Republic to keep the locals and visiting gringos happy. The duty free bottles leaving on every flight out of the Dominican Republic help to make the DR one of the most prosperous islands in the Caribbean. Tom glanced at his gold Omega Seamaster, Cindy's wedding gift, and announced, "Bottoms up," so they could get back to the hotel and join the women for a poolside night-cap. Tom passed around the fifty-dollar bill that he won from Ludwig and asked Carlos if American money was used much at the gallera and around town.

"Ludwig is the only one that uses it at the gallera. Around town tourists use it, but not big bills like Ludwig uses," Carlos answered. "All the stores like American money so they can make money on the exchange rate."

While Tom was digging a few crumpled pesos from his pocket to pay the bar bill, Carlos flagged down the next full size cruising Impala, euphemistically called a taxi, and told his buddy, the driver, to take his good friends to the Iberostar by the shortest route for the usual three-pesos fare. Tom waved his appreciation to Carlos through the dusty window as the smoking Impala lumbered away.

The men had no trouble locating their wives seated beside the now quiet pool awaiting their return from the bachelor party. Tom could tell that the usually reticent Neil was eager to share the cockfight happenings with the women so he just held hands with Cindy across the table while waiting for another Presidente to arrive. The wedding was scheduled for 6 PM tomorrow so he had plenty of time to sleep off the effects of his bachelor fling now happily turned co-ed.

Neil had the good sense to spare the gruesome, macabre details of the cockfights like dead cocks having their eyes pecked out, focusing more on the irrational crowd's frenzied betting and cheering behavior. But he couldn't resist telling about the dead cock in the final fight being kicked into the seats by the person, in a major temper tantrum, from whom Tom had just won fifty-dollars. The ladies were appalled that anyone could be so ill-tempered as to not have any respect for the dead rooster. The girls, wondering where were the PETA people when this act of cruelty took place, brought laughter from the men as indeed the basic premise of cockfighting would have been totally unacceptable to the PETA crowd.

The men took turns trying to explain what they knew about the foul-tempered kicker, acting like a spoiled child, based on their fragmentary information from Carlos: he was originally from Germany and arrived later than the original Jewish families who came to the Dominican Republic during the earlier stages of World War II. The Dominican Republic was the only Western hemisphere country to accept German refugees, giving them eighty acres of farmland near Sosua, a short distance from where they were at Puerto Plata. The early Jewish immigrants had initial concerns that they would be just trading one dictator, Hitler, for another, Trujillo, who ruled the Dominican Republic with an oppressive iron fist.

However, the industrious and hard working refugees with the blessing of the central government in Santo Domingo soon developed agricultural and dairy operations that are still prosperous years later. A few, like Ludwig, had been able to parlay their previous work experiences in Europe into similar jobs in the Dominican Republic. Ludwig, because of his family's many generations of brewing history in Germany, made the lucrative transition by becoming the manager of the local Brugal rum distillery, which placed him at the social and financial apex of this stretch of the northern coast of the Dominican Republic. There were medical people and other professionals that were able to use their skills in their new homeland and some refugees immigrated to other countries after the war ended.

Cindy could tell that the cockfight stories, enhanced by the Presidentes, were assuming the same mythological status that she had heard countless times when the boys relived past moments of their athletic pseudo-glory. She gave the girls a high-sign that she was going to the restroom.

The ladies were relieved to escape for a little feminine strategy session where they again agreed that tonight would not be the time to bring up their earlier beach altercation. Tonight, the men were best left undisturbed in their own fantasy world of triumphant gambling at the expense of a vanquished local hero. They returned to the table where they had been hardly missed and they not so subtly mentioned to their husbands that the bar was closed so they might as well retire to their rooms.

VIII

Ludwig surrendered his Mercedes 580's keys to his gatekeeper for the daily car wash to remove the salt spray from living so close to the ocean. His wife had left him a message that she would be home a little later and they could have dinner on their expansive deck to better enjoy the Caribbean sunset. Ludwig was not the romantic that his wife was and he always pragmatically commented, "If you miss tonight's sunset, there'll be another tomorrow."

He mixed himself a double shot of rum and coke using Brugal's select rum that was reserved for export to the lucrative German market. As Brugal's local plant manager and major stockholder, he had no problem maintaining his private supply as well as that of the rest of the close-knit Jewish community. When heading to the deck to read the international edition of the New York Times, he noticed his two cameras. The one with the long telephoto lens was where it was left nightly by the deck guard when he finished his daily duty of documenting naked trespassers on his private beach property. When the 36 shot roll of film was used-up, the guard dropped it off downtown for processing so Ludwig could examine the photo evidence, usually grainy and out of focus because of the distance to the offending party on the beach. Ludwig preferred to examine the prints from the second camera that were taken by the beach guard down at the beach. However, tonight that camera was on the table with its back open and the now worthless film unwinding on the table. The cryptic note taped to the bent and sprung camera back read, "Need a new camera. Will explain later."

Ludwig lived in the present, the only time frame that he could control, so he pushed the house security system alarm that brought his four on-duty security officers on the run with weapons drawn to his deck table. The unwinding 35 mm film became wrapped around his wrist as he angrily waved the broken camera for all to see, wanting an explanation from the cowering semicircle around the table. Finally, his head of security, Jimmie, explained that he had taken pictures of a partially naked trespasser that afternoon and then carried the camera with him to the Orange Mall to confront her with the evidence in the hope that she would pay their private fine without going to a threatened formal court hearing. Jimmie said that she must be some sort of karate expert as she kicked the camera out of his hands, springing it open as it hit the concrete.

Still entangled in the film Ludwig tried to launch the camera over the deck railing but the tag of film embedded in the camera's spool abruptly truncated its flight like a 12 gauge shotgun blasting an escaping mallard. Jimmie retrieved the camera and dutifully placed it back on the table, this time out of the reach of his still fuming boss.

This had not been a good afternoon for Ludwig starting with the public embarrassment of losing a prime fighting cock and the fifty-dollar bet to an obnoxious gringo. Now his specially ordered Leica built to his brother's professional photography specifications in the German Leica plant was trashed and the film with a week's worth of salacious evidence was worthless. Jimmie and the others inched back from the table to allow Ludwig a little latitude for his next outburst. Finally, Ludwig smiled at Jimmie and said, "Get the rum and some glasses."

Ludwig didn't often have a drink with his hired hands. However, today he felt the need to let his hair down with the men who watched his back-side as he had the intuition, based on his deeply engrained paranoia about issues that he could not control, that these two disparate events were somehow connected.

His over three decades living in the tropical paradise of the Dominican Republic had almost baked-out his memory of his former life back in Germany that caused him to secretly flee for his life. He was sure that no one still alive in the Dominican Republic knew his real migration story. The former local rabbi from a small town near his hospital SS posting at Dortmund who was instrumental in securing Ludwig's secret escape from Europe to the Dominican Republic, had died mysteriously three months after Ludwig arrived and he wasn't replaced for well over a year until an older German/Spanish-speaking rabbi could be found to come to the Dominican Republic.

After taking a year to settle into the small Jewish community at Sosua the new rabbi performed his first wedding uniting Ludwig and Naomi, the daughter of the deceased rabbi. Even though WWII was now over, no relatives of the bride or groom attended the wedding ceremony. Most of Naomi's family perished in the concentration camps and Ludwig was still out-of-touch with his family to prevent the authorities from tracing him to the Dominican Republic. Their honeymoon consisted of a quiet weekend at a beach hotel near them at Puerto Plata.

After being married to Naomi for over thirty years, Ludwig finally convinced himself that Naomi's father, the rabbi, had not revealed to her before his suspicious death, the true story of why her husband had to come to the Dominican Republic. Otherwise, she probably would not have married him in the first place or even stayed married to him all these years.

Their marriage produced two children, now living and working in the United States. The children attended elementary and high school at the exclusive Aiglon prep school in the mountains of Switzerland. This gave the children a world-wide circle of influential friends for their adult lives. During their school years in Switzerland, Ludwig never visited them. However, Naomi probably overcompensated by visiting the children for every major and many minor school functions. Naomi and the children gave up trying to persuade Ludwig to visit Aiglon as he always said that his work was too busy to leave. He never shared with his family or anyone else his true reason for not wishing to return to Europe, especially Germany: the fear that his previous SS life in Germany would be unmasked.

Ludwig insisted that the children attend colleges in the United States since that would give them the best chance for good jobs after graduation. He also insisted that they attend college near a large metropolitan area to provide some anonymity for him when he came to visit. Naomi reluctantly grew to accept Ludwig's obsession with privacy never knowing the reason for it. He always wanted to either avoid a crowd or, if confronted with one, then would get lost in it. Naomi and the children questioned, behind his back, this big city rationale for picking a college as he never visited them at their prep school in Switzerland and thus it was doubtful if he would visit them in college. Their years at Aiglon stimulated the two children's international interest, so they both attended Georgetown's renowned school of international affairs in Washington, D.C.

Their son, Bernardo was still in D.C. attending Georgetown Law School. He was hoping that his fluency in French and German from his Aiglon prep school days would help him find his niche in a large multi-national corporation when he graduated from law school.

Their daughter, Susana, married a successful options trader in Chicago shortly after her college graduation. The news of her pregnancy jump-started Naomi's grandparent instinct with many visits and shopping adventures planned even though they were a couple thousand miles apart.

Early on Ludwig often said to Naomi that the family should change their last name from Walther to a less Germanic name like Smith to disassociate themselves from the well-known German gun manufacturer, Walther, to whom they were not related. His real reason for wanting this name change, playing into his per-petual paranoia, was to add another layer of difficulty for anyone trying to track him down from his former SS days. However, as he was becoming more successful in his career, he put the name change issue on the back burner. His daughter's marriage obviated her need to change her name and Ludwig finally dropped the name change issue with his son when he started law school. Any family name change now would generate questions of why do it that Ludwig did not want to deal with as it could open the door of his own name change from Katz to Walther when he escaped from Europe to the Dominican Republic.

Naomi was always skeptical of the need for this name change knowing that Walther was not Ludwig's previous name in Germany. She knew that Ludwig's brother's name in Germany was not Walther, but Schanz. Her father, the rabbi, told her before his waterfall death that many refugees coming to the Dominican Republic had changed their names to facilitate their escape from Europe with new names and identities. Ludwig's security detail was charged with shielding Ludwig from everyone, even to a certain degree from members of their own small Jewish community of Sosua. They were especially on alert when visitors arrived from Germany or Israel who wanted to meet Ludwig under the guise of being old friends. Puerto Plata and the entire Dominican Republic were becoming very popular tourist destinations for European travelers, especially German Jews who wanted to visit Sosua as a tribute to those who escaped the holocaust.

For many years in the summer, Ludwig and Naomi, with only Jimmie as a bodyguard, would make a trip to neighboring Puerto Rico to vacation with his brother Konrad Schanz from Germany. Ludwig always chartered a private plane for the short, hopefully non-stop, flight to Aguada, the non-touristy but serious surfer-world at the western end of Puerto Rico. They stayed in the secluded ocean-side compound of the owner of the Ron Rico rum distillery, his friendly Caribbean rival. The estate's resident staff knew Ludwig as a rich liquor distributor from New York, who was to be extended every hospitality at the villa over-looking the world-famous Tres Palmas big wave beach.

In their younger days Ludwig and Naomi would paddle around the calm shallows on surfboards nervously watching their teenage son and daughter trying to conquer the walls of water crashing all around them. After dinner Ludwig and his brother would reminisce about their daredevil days of hiking-up and then skiing down uncharted Austrian mountains, even once out-skiing an advancing avalanche, so Naomi's maternal caution about the dangers of the big surf for their children fell on deaf ears. The year that Ludwig met his brother in Argentina to visit old military service friends from Germany was still a sore point with Naomi as she didn't know what was so important about the Argentina visit that they had to skip their Puerto Rico visit that summer.

Looking at the now worthless Leica, fortunately out of reach on the table across from him, Ludwig thought of all the damn trouble caused by that old work-horse of a camera. On one of their clandestine Puerto Rico surfing vacations, his brother used that very camera to take a telephoto shot of Bernardo and Susana about to be buried by the curl of a monster wave above their heads with he and Naomi sitting on their surfboards slightly out of focus in the foreground. Ludwig remembered going ballistic when his brother sent him a copy of the surfer magazine that saw fit to publish the dramatic photo under the caption, "Family Day at the Beach." The magazine's listed just the two kids names—Bernardo and Susana—as showing off for their parents at Tres Palmas beach in Puerto Rico. Naomi did not understand Ludwig's anger and why the two brothers had no contact for months after this stunning photo appeared. Ludwig reluctantly acknowledged his family's identity in the picture when his Puerto Rican host called to congratulate him about making the surfer magazine centerfold.

IX

Since Cindy and Tom wanted a small, personal wedding they decided to import their own priest for the ceremony. The Iberostar's rent-a-collar minister couldn't provide the intimacy they were seeking so they invited Fr. Dennis, Tom's college seminary roommate. Dennis was privy to Tom's soul searching and ultimately the heart-rending decision to leave behind his childhood dream of becoming a priest. Dennis knew from the instant that Tom excitedly burst into their college dormitory room and told him that he just had a coke break wearing his Roman collar and black cassock with the only girl in their cosmology class, that things were going to change in Tom's life. When he asked Tom what they talked about, Tom couldn't remember and his comment that it didn't really matter was a red flag that Tom's celibate mind was being over-taken by his love-starved heart. The heart usually wins these primal struggles. Tom did remember that the girl's name was Cindy, the same Cindy who would be standing in the sand facing him to be married by his best friend.

Dennis had continued his seminary studies in Rome before being ordained a priest while Tom easily passed the thorough background and security checks prior to starting the elite secret service training regimen. The two friends stayed in touch through the years, playing golf a couple times a year as their schedules permitted. Fr. Dennis arrived the day after the bachelor party at the cockfight, which was the lunch time topic of the men's highly animated conversation. So vivid were Tom's, Neil's, and David's descriptions of the cockfights, that Fr. Dennis felt like he had been there. His offer to hear Ludwig's confession for abusing the dead rooster with his angry kick brought raucous laughter from the guys at the lunch table who viewed Ludwig as the perfect non-candidate for any kind of repentance. The ladies were too occupied with getting their beautiful wedding look to bother with lunch with the guys.

The 6 o'clock wedding time arrived with the wedding party ready for the beach side ceremony. Cindy's scripted wedding vows were short and not overly sweet or romantic. Fr. Dennis was a naturally gifted preacher who knew when not to try to one-up the simple ceremony under the colorful canopy on the beautiful Caribbean shore. The ceremony was over in less than 15 minutes, and Tom prudently didn't insist on including the Bible reading that exhorted the wife to be subservient to her husband. When Fr. Dennis concluded with the announcement that the bride and groom could now kiss, Tom embraced Cindy with a new-found passion. Finally, Fr. Dennis announced to the laughter of all, "You two better come up for air."

The dinner reception for the wedding party was in full swing in a colorful pool-side lanai with sheer repand valances that was the Dominican Republic's answer to a Las Vegas wedding chapel. After the wedding toasts, while waiting for the food to be served, Carlos, now smartly uniformed as the hotel's concierge unlike his casual dress at the cockfights, was nervously rocking from foot to foot. When he caught Tom's ever-vigilant eye, Tom detected a sense of urgency in his demeanor, so he excused himself to see what was so important that it couldn't wait until after their wedding dinner.

Tom knew it couldn't be a work related issue as he was too far down the totem pole at his Treasury Department job to merit an international call while on vacation. Carlos said that he really needed to talk to the ladies, especially the one who beat up the cop yesterday at the Orange Mall. This angry cop was now waiting at the front desk with another policeman and they were not going to leave until the ladies came to the desk. Carlos warned apologetically that the police would come in to get the women if they didn't voluntarily come out.

Tom held up a finger, telling Carlos that he needed a minute to find out what the women's problem was yesterday. The men at their bachelor party were supposed to be the ones on a short leash so Tom couldn't fathom the women getting into trouble on their short shopping excursion up the beach. The women's feminine intuition sensed that the concierge's visit involved them and they started approaching Tom, who just threw up his hands as if to say, 'What the hell is going on?'

The six of them formed a circle with Fr. Dennis on the fringe. Cindy, probably because it was her day and she was wearing the dress to prove it, started to explain yesterday's Orange Mall incident, but Joanne interrupted her as she was the guilty party. She explained that they walked past many topless women on the beach on the way to the Orange Mall and she assumed it was legal. Mary chimed in that going topless is not illegal in the Dominican Republic except private property owners have the right to forbid it on their property. They had apparently crossed onto private property where it is illegal to be topless. Hence the requested confrontation in the hotel's lobby with the officers from the Orange Mall was now interrupting Cindy's day.

Joanne smiled and gave her husband Neil a high five as she explained and partially demonstrated her disabling knee to the groin of her attacker. The others didn't smile as the gravity of the situation started to hit them. Carlos entered the circle and interrupted with the plea to meet the police at the desk or very soon they would come inside and seize the guilty party. Cindy as she stroked crumbs off her wedding dress said that she couldn't go to meet the officers dressed like this, but everyone else said that it was the perfect diversion. Maybe it would inspire leniency. Tom told their waiter to hold their meals as they would be right back.

The wedding party lagged behind the hurrying concierge, as Cindy tried to avoid tripping on her long wedding gown. Just before turning into the open air hotel lobby, David stopped everyone and announced that he and his wife Mary, both attorneys, would do the talking and no one was to admit or sign anything until he or Mary had a chance to approve.

The original two officers had grown to four to the dismay of Carlos. Obviously, the authorities expected a problem. The men immediately recognized two of the four that were Ludwig's bodyguards at yesterday's cockfight. The women recognized the other two from the Orange Mall. Tom noticed that one of the uniforms was different than the other three and this one seemed to be the real thing with a numbered badge on his shirt pocket and a gun on his belt. The real officer unsnapped the strap holding his pistol in its holster and kept his hand resting on the pistol grip, which got Tom's complete attention. Tom and Neil went to either end of their semicircle facing the cops so that one of them might have a chance at getting to the shooter if things deteriorated that far. David and Mary stayed in the center of their semicircle so that they could better face the officer talking from the center of the four uninvited visitors.

The private guard, who was still hunched over when the girls hurriedly left the Orange Mall yesterday, was now standing erect, but unfortunately not in a very good mood as he threw the open-backed camera at Joanne's feet. "You broke this expensive camera yesterday. It's also a family keepsake of Ludwig, my boss. He's very mad at you."

"Him, mad at me! I'm really pissed at him for making you take pictures of partially clothed women for his private collection. At the very least he deserves a broken camera!"

Neil, as chief CIA training instructor, hadn't seen his wife this provoked since her final week of CIA training when any and all intimidating harassment was used to break the trainees. Neil quickly glanced toward Tom at the opposite end of their semicircle without taking his focus off the officer with his hand on the gun. Neil sensed the need to quickly defuse this petty conflict before it escalated into an international incident. He didn't wait for lawyers David and Mary to open their legal bag of tricks. Holding his hands up as a sign of surrender he slid sideways placing himself between his wife and the paunchy accuser. The officer with the gun seemed to stiffen a little but didn't draw his weapon. Neil hoped that the other officers recognized them from the cockfight but that wasn't necessarily a good thing since Tom had publicly bested Ludwig. Neil broke the tense silence with an offer to pay for the broken camera right on the spot as he removed a bulging money clip from his pocket.

The real police officer with his hand still on the gun held up his other hand with the order, "Stop." Everyone took a deep breath. One of the big goons from the cockfight waved a thick envelop in Joanne's direction. "We have papers for your arrest. Since you are Americans, and America is our friend, we will not arrest you tonight. However, the guilty lady must come with me to talk to the owner whose property was violated. We go now."

Out of the corner of his eye Tom caught Neil shaking his head no to this unusual request.

David stepped toward the still waving papers. "I'm a lawyer. May I please see the papers?"

The officer retracted the papers. "They're in Spanish. Do you know Spanish?"

"No, but my wife does, and she's a lawyer too."

"You can see the papers after the guilty lady goes to see my boss, whose property was violated."

Tom, as the de-facto leader of this beleaguered group, moved front and center not really knowing what he was going to say or do. Fortunately he was saved by Fr. Dennis still wearing his Roman collar. Father suspected that the four officers were Catholic because of the Dominican Republic's Spanish origins, so he decided to play the faith card. "With the permission of your bishop, I just married this couple, needlessly pointing to Cindy and Tom dressed in their wedding attire. We just started the reception with a special blessing from the pope. Won't you allow us to go back and finish our special wedding dinner?"

Pretty priestly stuff Tom thought to himself. Sure beats a back-alley rumble in your wedding attire! Tom could see the four men looking at each other, not knowing what to do. For sure they didn't want to incur the wrath of God by brushing aside a priest with the simple request of allowing the wedding festivities to go on.

The lead officer grabbed the papers and stuffed them under his arm, re-snapped the leather strap over the pistol's handle and picked up the camera. Looking at Joanne he ordered, "7 o'clock, tomorrow evening. You come to settle this serious complaint or you go to jail. Carlos will bring you."

The wedding party had to elbow their way through the circle of curious spectators that congregated in the lobby to observe this unexpected floor show. When they arrived back at their cozy lanai their dinners were cold. Tom learned years ago in the Washington, D.C. petty political games that you only fight the battles that you can win. Warm dinners were not a battle he could win in this laid-back Caribbean environment, so he proposed a toast to tomorrow's visit with Ludwig.

The loud reggae music being played through the pool-side speakers finally caused the wedding party to call it a night. The men agreed to meet for a 7 AM breakfast so the women could get an extra hour of beauty sleep. Fr. Dennis' tongue-in-cheek offer to say a 6 AM mass was met with silence until Tom mentioned that they could talk about it at breakfast, which was later than the proposed mass time.

• • • •

Tom found the pay phone in the lobby before the others came down the next morning. He used his Department of Treasury issued international calling card to place a call to the State

Department's 24-hour hotline where he was transferred to the Caribbean desk. He explained the situation to the flabbergasted analyst with the request that they request the American ambassador in the Dominican Republic capital of Santo Domingo be in touch with the local authorities in Puerto Plata to make these silly charges go away.

Tom had a gut feeling that something else was going on in this making a mountain of a mole hill by Ludwig working hand-in-hand with the local police, so he placed a second call to CIA headquarters in Langley. The director of covert operations was his classmate at the CIA training center called the Farm and Tom was always reluctant to push his friendship too far, especially for something as trivial as Joanne's topless beach stroll. His friend teased him about being too late as Neil and Joanne had already informed him of their dilemma. They jokingly decided that it was not necessary to dispatch a CIA plane to immediately extricate the guilty party, as no one's life seemed to be endangered. Tom's final request was for the CIA to do their most intensive Class IV background check of Ludwig Walther, as he always liked to know as much as he could about an adversary before he confronted him.

When the ladies finally joined the well-caffeinated men at the breakfast table, a plan for the day was worked out. Cindy wanted to take Joanne and Mary into the modest shopping area of Puerto Plata for their wedding attendant gifts since the Orange Mall shopping spree ended in the disaster that they were going to address later that night at Ludwig's house. Fr. Dennis and David offered to accompany the ladies to keep them out of trouble. Cindy, extolling the beauties of the native amber and Larimar jewelry that's unique to the Dominican Republic, provided unneeded encouragement for the day's shopping entertainment.

Tom and Neil were delighted to stay behind and enjoy some manly beach activities along with being back in touch with the State Department and the CIA at Langley. A beach volley ball left them hot and sweaty, so they jumped on jet skis to cool off as well as to get away from the beach crowd, some of whom Tom was sure recognized him from last night's lobby fiasco. They headed toward the Orange Mall, which was like a desert mirage against the cloudless blue sky. Half-way there on the bouncing jet skis, they noticed the large house in an estate setting that he assumed was where they were going tonight. They drove the jet skis far enough up on the beach to keep them from floating back out to sea. As they sat on their machines admiring the natural beauty of the ocean on one side and the man- made splendor of Ludwig's estate on the other, they detected someone at the top of the barrier bluff taking pictures of them with a telephoto lens. Obviously having taken enough pictures, he started to slip and slide in the sand of the sloping dune. He was talking on his walkie-talkie as he headed in their direction.

"Unless we want a second issue to deal with tonight, we'd better get our butts out of here," Neil said as he tugged on his jet ski to get it back into the water.

"He looks like one of the bozos from last night, but let's not stay around to find out," Tom replied. "I'm sure we'll see him again tonight."

They ran the jet skis out a couple hundred yards off shore and killed the engines. They could see the guard as he trudged back up the sandy slope struggling to get back to his observation area. "Ludwig sure has a bug up his butt about people on his beach," Tom commented as he restarted his engine. "Let's go pull up by the other jet skis at the Orange Mall and see where the girls caused all the ruckus."

Tom and Neil kept their life vests on, not trusting the natives if they left them with the jet skis. Even if they wanted to, they couldn't buy anything as they had left their money back at the hotel. They were on a post-facto scouting mission for any information that might be needed for tonight's meeting with Ludwig. They saw an older security officer aimlessly wandering between the colorful stalls of overpriced merchandise. Neil thought that it was a good thing Joanne had not kneed this septuagenarian in the groin; otherwise they could be facing a homicide charge. They both noticed the closeness of the stalls and booths, so there had to be many witnesses of the girl's confrontation, which could be a good or bad thing depending on who paid the witnesses the most.

Their slow cruise back to the hotel in the shallows near the shore caused the camera with the telephoto lens to be again aimed at them. Tom was tempted to flip off the pervert behind the camera, but for the sake of international relations he thought better. Their proximity to the sunbathers on the beach allowed them to see a number of ladies enjoying the sun in the European topless mode, so what Joanne did would appear to be legal as nowhere was it posted as forbidden on Ludwig's property. If she were illegal, then the authorities would have to arrest half the women on the beach.

Back at the Iberostar resort to change out of their wet swimsuits, they had messages to call two numbers that they recognized as the State Department and the CIA at Langley. The State Department call got the typical bureaucratic response that the ambassador would be in touch with the proper Dominican authorities and that in the meanwhile don't do anything to exacerbate the current situation. No problem Tom thought, as long as they keep their hands and cameras off us, especially the ladies.

The CIA was apologetic that they did not have time to do a complete background check of Ludwig Walther in the few hours since Tom's earlier call. Turning the clock backward they ran into a dead-end street before 1945 when he arrived in the Dominican Republic as a young man. The usual boiler plate biographical background of the last few years of Ludwig's very successful life was informative but contained nothing unusual except for one finding. Ten years ago a complaint was filed by an animal rights organization that was dismissed by the local Dominican Republic court. Tom was not too surprised by this complaint based on seeing Ludwig kick the dead rooster at the cockfight and he assumed it probably concerned Ludwig's involvement with the cockfighting sport, especially his raising of prize roosters. He figured that any complaints about the rooster farms were probably similar to the veal raising controversy that never seemed to generate much traction with the apathetic public who liked their veal regardless of how it was produced. Cockfighting was an entrenched tradition in the Dominican Republic society just like baseball. The courts would be foolhardy to tamper with it, especially since such a prominent citizen had a stake in it.

Tom's tense, "What the hell was that complaint all about?" put the briefer on the other end of the line in a defensive mode. The complaint, filled by a dismissed worker at Ludwig's rooster farm, alleged that Ludwig kept a colony of monkeys in unsanitary cages. Furthermore, he would often put a muzzled, hence defenseless, baby monkey in a training cage with a maturing rooster to teach the rooster the aggression needed to survive in the real cockfighting pit by chasing and continuously pecking the retreating monkey.

. . . .

Apparently Ludwig didn't want the baby monkey to be killed in its first encounter with a fighting cock. If seriously injured, it would be doped up with morphine and a few days later put back in a cage with another cock. Usually the second and subsequent times the muzzled monkey would be more aggressive but still could only feebly fight back trying to fend off the fierce onslaught of the rooster. Tom's image of cute baby monkeys being cuddled by their mothers was erased by this bloody baby monkey slaughter at a rooster boot-camp.

After getting off the phone from these Washington calls, Tom and Neil sat at the poolside bar, awaiting the return of the downtown shoppers. There were moments of silence that only good friends can endure without the need for constant chatter. Neil understood that when Tom was silent, he was thinking serious thoughts. When they did converse, they were both getting more frustrated by the minute at the absurdity of their predicament. They knew that law enforcement procedures in third world countries could be different than in the United States, especially when the town's most prominent citizen with his own private guards seemed to have the official police also working for him. "Perhaps a good example of pesos talking," Tom said to break one bout of silence.

They agreed that tonight's meeting with Ludwig could be interesting, especially if their calls to Washington were not relayed to the local Dominican authorities.

Nursing their rum and cokes, they looked across the pool at the commotion in the lobby as the returned shoppers were giddily showing their wares to the smiling desk clerks. Then the shoppers noticed Tom and Neil waving at them from the bar. Tom's under his breath comment, "Looks like we'll get to check the damage too," brought a reluctant nod from Neil. They gushed over the Larimar necklaces that Cindy bought as gifts for Joanne and Mary. The blue Larimar stones are mined near Puerto Plata and are unique to the Dominican Republic. Cindy explained that the Larimar is considered a healing stone and when worn around the neck is believed to impart increased talking and communication ability. David commented, "This stone should be the patron stone of lawyers so they'll never be lost for words."

Fr. Dennis' retort, "Don't forget about priests," brought a round of high fives as the group dispersed to get dressed for the night's big meeting with Ludwig.

X

Shortly before 7 PM, the seven of them loaded into the newer of the Iberostar's white Econoline vans for the short trip to Ludwig's requested, nay required, meeting at his near-by estate. Fr. Dennis being the odd man sat in the passenger seat as if he were the tour director. He was wearing his Roman collar to gain a little more credence with the native Dominicans in case he had to play the Catholic card again. The van's air conditioning hardly had time to kick in before they stopped at the guard-house half-way up Ludwig's long driveway. A uniformed guard walked around the van glancing in the windows with a dog on a leash sniffing at the vehicle's undercarriage. Back at the driver's window he asked, "What are all these people doing here?"

Fr. Dennis leaned across toward the open window, pointing to his watch. "Your boss wanted us to be here at 7 o'clock tonight."

"No, he told me that only one woman was coming, not a van full of people."

Fr. Dennis turned and tossed the hot potato into Tom's lap, sitting in the row behind, who quickly replied, "His man didn't say only one person so we're all here to see Ludwig."

The guard scanned the inside of the van counting seven visitors. He spun on his heels and reentered the guard-house. They could see him talking on the phone. Momentarily, a black sedan came speeding toward them and skidded sideways to block the driveway beyond the guard-house, obviously a sign of serious trouble. So Tom told everyone, "Remember that we're all in this together and to remain calm," which became difficult when they saw three armed men jump out of the car and the guard reemerge from his guard-house with a shotgun aimed at the van.

They were ordered out of the van and told to put their hands above their heads on the side of the van so they could be frisked. David mumbled that this was a violation of their constitutional rights. Tom told him to shut up and do what he was told if he wanted to live to tell about it. After the frisker was through and shouted his professional opinion that all was clear, they were ordered to turn around with their backs to the van.

The driver emerged from the sideways car. He was immediately recognized as Ludwig, the object of their visit. He gave a dismissive wave to his guards who lowered their weapons and retreated. He walked to the driver's side door and spoke loudly enough for all to hear. "Carlos, you should have alerted me that you were bringing all of them. You know I can't allow this many people at my house unannounced. The world is full of bad people, even here in this Dominican paradise. Only the guilty woman was required to visit," he said, waving a roll of crumpled papers.

"We do everything as a group," Tom replied with the implied firmness that no one, especially one of the ladies, was going to be sent over to Ludwig's house alone. "We'd be happy to jump back in the van and return to the hotel."

"Impossible, since we still have this paper work from the police. Plus we have a new trespassing complaint from this afternoon involving two of you on jet skis. Follow me back to the house."

The seven reloaded into the van for the short ride to the house. "This is all bull shit," David screamed. "We should sue the ass-hole."

"Thanks for your expert legal opinion," Neil said. "I'd rather do a covert mission and take out the arrogant bastard."

Tom silenced everyone. "Let's keep our cool. This game's being played in his ballpark, by his rules. Father, why don't you ride back to the hotel with Ludwig's friend, Carlos, since this doesn't involve you?"

"Not a chance. I'm having too much fun being with my crazy, wild friends."

Ludwig, with his bone-rimmed Prada sunglasses resting on his thinning hair, was at the front door to greet them. They followed him into what he called the glass room and took seats on large sofas facing the ocean.

"Could I please see the papers?" David asked. Ludwig ignored him as he retrieved a small monkey named Kraut from a floor-to- ceiling cage in the back of the room. The monkey perched on his shoulder and chirped his welcome at the visitors. The monkey dislodged the sunglasses and Ludwig attempted to catch them in mid-air. The sound of the breaking lenses hitting the hard tile floor elicited a verbal response of, "Damned monkey," as well as a kick that sent the frames bouncing off a sliding glass cabinet door.

"Does he bite?" Cindy asked as she snuggled closer to Tom.

"Only unfriendly visitors. He's young, only been here a few months," a smiling Ludwig answered as he took a seat facing his guests. "Are you going to the cockfights tomorrow?" he asked, looking daggers at Tom.

"If we do, we'll have holy reinforcements," Tom replied, gesturing toward Fr. Dennis, while looking sternly back at Ludwig's two different color eyes. One eye was blue and the other was dark brown, almost black.

"I don't like losing, especially when it was my best rooster in the ring. I'd like a chance to get even."

"Beginner's luck," Tom countered. "Sometime you'll have to explain the fine points of cockfighting to us, especially how the roosters are trained to fight."

"You don't need to know any more. That's the most I've lost in years. Never again, especially to a first-time gringo," Ludwig said, patting his monkey's back.

The group collectively relaxed during this diversionary skirmish.

Wine was offered. Tom, noting that the bottles of light and dark wine bore labels from Germany, proposed a toast to his host in halting German. When Ludwig raised his glass of wine, Tom again noticed the dark scar on the top of his left forearm and also the less obvious scar on the inside of his upper arm that disappeared into his armpit when his arm was lowered. Years ago a dermatome-like razor must have been used to remove a thickness of skin on his forearm that left a dark bumpy keloid scar that must be just as unsightly as the original problem that required the surgery.

Ludwig interrupted the developing congeniality by picking up the broken camera with the still-attached exposed film and the roll of papers from an end table next to his chair. "Which one of you ladies was walking on my beach?"

"We all were," Cindy replied.

"You know what I mean, naked."

Neil, in defense of his unidentified wife, jumped up and approached within inches of Ludwig. Pointing to his feet, he said, "Your guards didn't discover my most lethal weapon. One kick and two necks are broken. Is that what you want, you ass-hole?" Teeth gritted, Neil backed slightly away to give himself more kicking room to take out the monkey before his foot hit Ludwig. The rest of the group sat on the edge of the sofas.

Ludwig unrolled the crumpled papers and started ripping them into narrow strips. Neil moved away a couple more steps. Ludwig threw the shreds of paper into the air behind his chair in the direction of his broken sunglasses. "The camera and film are destroyed so I have no evidence. Case dismissed." Tom noticed a contorted angry smile, like after the cockfight, cross Ludwig's face.

Neil figured that since they were on a roll he would clear the slate. "No problem with the jet skis, either?"

"I have pictures of you pulled up on my beach, but you're right. No problem with the jet skis."

Neil sat back down and gave Joanne a relieved hug. Neil was unaware that great political pressure had been applied by the Dominican government on Ludwig after Tom and Neil's calls to

Washington asking for help from the Dominican Capital at Santo Domingo. They were also unaware that Ludwig had never filed a similar complaint with the local Puerto Plata courts so Neil's macho defense of his wife was superfluous. Nevertheless, a duly chastised Ludwig offered to give his guests a tour of his ocean-side mansion. Tom had his reasons to see as much of Ludwig's lair as he could, but he didn't want to appear overly anxious. "Maybe just a short tour, while we wait for Carlos to pick us up. By the way, Ludwig, we offered to pay for the broken camera."

"Money can't replace this custom-made Leica, especially the quality old German lens. It was a gift from my brother in Germany years ago. Let's go on the tour," Ludwig said, obviously proud to show off his show-place home.

The women were especially interested in the spotless kitchens, the everyday one on the first floor and the larger stainless steel commercial one on the lower level. Ludwig took pleasure in showing off the sleek European appliances and gadgets that the women had only seen pictures of in gourmet cooking magazines.

Back in the hallway, Tom noticed a door that was open a crack that led to a bathroom. "Mind if I use the rest room here?" Tom surprised Ludwig. Ludwig flicked his hand toward the door and Tom went inside while the rest of the group continued down the hall.

Tom didn't bother to lock the door as he didn't want the locking sound to alert Ludwig that he might be doing anything besides using the facilities for their designed purpose. He opened the mirror door above the sink that exposed the contents of the medicine cabinet. There were a number of prescription bottles on the shelf that he turned their labels toward him. He flushed the toilet and then took close-up pictures of the prescription bottles with his small pocket camera. He randomly rotated the bottles before closing the mirror door. He wet his hands under the sink faucet and left the neatly folded towel awkwardly hanging on the gold towel bar.

Tom was still rubbing his hands together in a drying mode as he caught up with the group in a small sitting room down the hall. The young monkey whose name was Kraut enjoyed the attention he was getting during the tour. Tom discretely checked out the expensive wall decorations and an extensive Hummel figurine collection and a few gold-embossed leather bound books on the ultra contemporary glass bookshelves.

Fr. Dennis got the group's attention when he pointed to an old leather bound volume with a German title. "Ludwig, excuse me, can I ask a question?"

"Of course."

"I studied theology under Hans Kung in Germany and learned enough German to be dangerous. Isn't that an old leather bound volume of Mein Kampf?" Tom noticed the two small silver baby mugs that were resting up against the aging volume in a valiant effort to be bookends.

"Indeed it is," Ludwig proudly replied.

"I remember one of our professors telling us that Hitler only had 100 copies thus bound and printed as gifts for his best friends. It looks like you have copy 99 of Hitler's autobiography."

"I don't know about only 100 copies. It's one of my most cherished possessions from my father," Ludwig said, anxious to keep the tour moving.

Tom nodded his approval to Fr. Dennis as they both sensed Ludwig's uneasiness about Fr. Dennis' bookshelf discovery. Tom made a mental note of the engravings on the cups. On one cup he could read October 3, 1949 and on the other cup only the year 1951 was visible.

Tom was hoping to see Ludwig's office or private study to get the true measure of the man. However, a number of unopened doors hid these and other personal rooms from his inquisitive mind.

Carlos had the cooled van waiting for them under the mansion's porte-cochere. From the back row David spoke loudly enough for Fr. Dennis and Carlos in the front seats to hear. "After Neil got Ludwig's attention, the thing that I enjoyed most was the monkey."

"Which one?" Tom wondered, putting his finger to his lips as a signal for all to be quiet until they were out of the van away from Carlos.

"Very funny, Tom! We could have been killed in there and not by the real monkey," David answered.

Since they were staying at an all-inclusive resort, it was the perpetual joke whose turn it was to buy a round of drinks. Fr. Dennis offered to buy this nightcap round of 'holy water' at the pool-side bar, where the bartender was on a first name basis with at least the men in the party.

Neil, the hero of the evening, was unusually quiet and withdrawn until his wife Joanne proposed a toast to her savior, who rescued her from the grasp of a photographic sex pervert. Neil let that notion hang out there for a moment after the toast before he asked everyone what they thought of Ludwig. He was especially interested in the ladies' and Fr. Dennis' opinions since they had not seen Ludwig's performance at the cockfight.

To a person they wondered where Ludwig's wife was or if she even lived there. However, they finally agreed that she must live there at least some of-the-time; otherwise the kitchens wouldn't be in such fine order with nothing out of place.

Tom commented that the wife had to live there as he saw prescription bottles with her name on them when he used the bathroom during their house tour.

"You snooped in their drawers?" Cindy indignantly shouted at Tom.

"No, I didn't open their drawers—just the medicine cabinet door above the sink," Tom said, with a proud smirk on his face.

Tom could see smoke coming from his new wife's ears at what he thought was a harmless confession.

"Even though what you learned is illegal and not admissible in a court of law, what did you learn?" David questioned in his most judicial manner.

"I only remember three prescription bottles. One was for a female hormone that Naomi is taking. The other two were for Ludwig: a small eye-drop bottle and a bigger pill bottle of Morphine." Glancing at a still simmering Cindy, Tom thought it not wise to mention that he took pictures of the medicine cabinet contents. Soon enough this would come to her attention after the film was developed back home.

To shift the focus from his illegal medicine cabinet search, Tom mentioned the picture wall where he saw a faded but dated family portrait showing Ludwig, a woman, a boy and a girl, professionally taken at one of the Disney World Kodak picture spots with Cinderella's castle in the background all decked-out for Christmas. Ludwig, wearing aviator Ray Bans, jacket collar turned up and hat tilted over his face, was barely recognizable hidden in the shadows behind his wife and two children.

Neil confessed that he almost didn't get his vis-a-vis tirade started because he immediately noticed that the pet monkey had only one eye and its face and arms were riddled with scars too numerous to count. Mary asked if he was sure about the one eye business. Dave jumped in saying that he noticed the same thing as one eye never opened and it had a depressed eye socket indicative of no eyeball being present. Tom and Neil glanced at each and silently agreed that tonight wasn't the time to explain Ludwig's probable brutal cock training methods that caused the young monkey's disfigurement.

Showing her CIA trained power of observation, Joanne questioned, "Speaking of eyes, did anyone notice that Ludwig's eyes are two different colors? One is a beautiful light blue and the other is dark brown, nearly black."

Tom took the bait as he had noticed it. "Which eye is which color?"

"What the hell difference does that make?" Cindy snapped, frustrated that her new husband couldn't leave his job behind on their honeymoon.

"The right eye is blue. One guess what eye is dark brown?" Joanne commented to the laughter of all, trying to dissipate the newlyweds' tension.

As the evening cooled with the setting sun, Tom worked up the courage to ask if any of the ladies wanted to go to the cockfight tomorrow afternoon, especially since Ludwig had asked if they were going. Cindy knew that Tom was up to something and was obtusely asking her permission to go without really wanting the ladies to go. If she wanted to watch Tom squirm out of his skin, she would say yes to this pseudo invitation. However, she noticed the other two ladies vigorously shaking their heads no, so she was relieved to tell Tom to do some more male bonding while the ladies would either go for another beach walk, this time clothed, to the Orange Mall to finish their rudely interrupted previous shopping adventure. If they felt adventuresome they could visit the adjoining Jewish town of Sosua.

XI

Tom and Neil were having their early breakfast trying to digest last night's bizarre encounter with Ludwig and relate it to the background information that they had received from Washington. Soon they were joined by David and Fr. Dennis.

Tom filled everyone in on the old complaint against Ludwig for cruelty to monkeys, which involved using them as sacrificial sparing partners in the training of his fighting roosters. When Ludwig agreed to cease and desist from this cruel practice, the complaint was dismissed.

"How old was that monkey on his shoulder?" David asked.

"Around one year old, based on my many trips from the seminary to the nearby Washington Zoo," Fr. Dennis answered. "The primate exhibit was my favorite, a chance to meet the relatives."

"It's obvious that he hasn't ceased and desisted from this gruesome training practice, otherwise that young monkey wouldn't be blind in one eye with a face-full of gouges. We should file another complaint," David threatened.

"Kraut's injuries appear like those in the old complaint, but I'm most concerned about the reddish bumps going up both the monkey's forearms, just like a street junkie. I saw them close up when I first got in Ludwig's face," Neil said.

"Morphine or heroin?" David wondered.

"Doesn't matter. Powerful illegal drugs are in the house or at the training farm. A more appropriate question might be, who else is using them? Maybe his wife was spaced out in bed—in no condition to see us," Neil conjectured.

"Is that scar on Ludwig's forearm from drug use?" David questioned.

"If so, it's not from recent drug usage as the scar looks old, probably from a previous surgery. I didn't see any tracks on his arms, but of course there are other areas of the body where drugs can be injected," Tom mentioned. "Maybe Kraut and Ludwig are sharing the same morphine prescription in the medicine cabinet. Probably the most puzzling thing is something that didn't happen during our visit."

"And that would be?" David asked.

"Where was his vaunted security, especially when Neil got in his face and threatened to kill him? The security was absent by design. Ludwig played us for a bunch of dummies. He knew that we wouldn't hurt him, and he was just toying with us before he tore up the charges. After my calls to Washington, some Dominican governmental higher-up must have told him to stop hassling us. Obviously, he still wanted one last run at us, probably trying to get even for his cockfight losses."

"That bastard!" Neil shouted. "I got my blood pressure up and nearly took him out for no reason. He and Kraut probably laughed themselves to sleep after we left. Now it's our turn to get even. For sure let's go to the cockfight."

While the others were cursing out the devious Ludwig and planning a strategy for the cockfight, Tom slipped away to the lobby to place a call to Langley. He hoped that he didn't send the CIA on a wild goose chase when he asked them to find out the names of the family of four that had their picture taken a year ago on December 22, at 11:30AM in front of Cinderella's castle at Disney World. He was sure that Disney World archived these old photos taken at a Kodak Picture

Spot in case someone wanted a copy at a later date. Once they had a name from the photos, he asked Langley to track down the family's hotel reservations as well as any other personal information, including credit cards. After he hung up the phone, he smiled and thought how great it was to have the powers of the federal government on his side as he tried to answer his questions about Ludwig.

Gleason couldn't get his mind around the fact that Ludwig still continued his monkey abuse with Kraut as exhibit A after his previous encounter with the Dominican authorities when he was ordered to stop using young monkeys as training foils for his young roosters. It probably was a sign that he had the local authorities under his influence so he could operate outside the law when it served his purposes.

Carlos, as the morning concierge, was making his rounds of the few early breakfast eaters when he stopped at their table. "What time are you going to the cockfights?"

The men looked at each other with the same question on their mind. "How did Carlos know that we going to the cockfights?"

'Ludwig,' Tom thought but didn't express it, as he avoided Carlos' question with a question. "What's the deal with the tours of the Brugal distillery? Do they offer free sample?"

"No free rum samples, but the Brugal plant is open everyday at 9 o'clock. Do you want to tour this morning before the cockfights? Our van can drop you off."

Tom made the executive decision that they would like to be there when the tours start at 9 AM. The others nodded in agreement.

"I can also meet you again at the cockfights," Carlos offered.

Fr. Dennis commented that he would appreciate all the betting tips that Carlos could provide.

Carlos asked if the women wanted to come on the Brugal tour also. Neil said that he doubted if his wife would ever want anything to do with Ludwig again as he probably still had her topless pictures from the other camera. Carlos told them to be in the lobby at 8:45 for the van to the Brugal plant tour and that he would see them later at the gallera for the cockfights.

. . . .

As Neil predicted, the women opted out of the Brugal distillery tour. Joanne's comment that she never wanted to see that creep Ludwig again left no doubt about how she felt. Cindy gave Tom a warning not to trust Ludwig as she was getting bad vibes from him. Mary and David, the two lawyers, agreed to start taking notes on their final few days in the Dominican Republic. Fr. Dennis thanked his celibacy for the simplicity of his solo decision to just go along with whatever the other guys were planning to do.

The Iberostar van dropped them off for the 9 o'clock tour, not at the visitors' entrance where a line was already forming, but at the employee entrance where they noticed Ludwig's parked Mercedes that had nearly run them over last night.

The men were disappointed in the tour as it only involved circling above the shipping and receiving department on an elevated walkway. They could barely see through steamed covered windows into the large distilling room where large vats were interconnected with pipes snaking in all directions. Prominent NO PHOTOS signs were needlessly posted along the walkway as no picture would turn out through the foggy windows.

The short tour conveniently ended in the company store where all of Brugal's products were for sale, not just those made in this plant. Tom's ulterior motive for wanting to take the tour became apparent when he loaded bottles of specially packaged Brugal Select into his shopping basket as gifts for his wedding party. When they were approaching the cash register, Ludwig came through a door at the end of the counter. "Do we get the friends and family discount?" Tom teased.

"Are you sure that you can afford this premium rum?" Ludwig countered, eying the bottles near the cash register.

"Only if you let us win again at the cockfights this afternoon," Tom replied to the somber Ludwig, who was vigorously shaking his head "no" to Tom's taunt. Tom wanted to use America dollars to avoid a paper trail for this much booze in case the image conscious Secret Service ever wanted to check his credit card records. Tom stopped the cashier who was starting to count out many small pesos bills with the request for his change in American dollars. She glanced at Ludwig with a helpless look as she didn't have large American bills to give back as change. Ludwig peeled a Fifty-dollar bill from his money clip for the cashier to use.

"I hope you have more of these to give us at the cockfights this afternoon," Tom said.

"You be sure to bring this fifty to the cockfight. I want it back." Ludwig reached across the counter to shake hands and to thank them for taking the Brugal tour. "See you this afternoon."

XII

After eating lunch at the Iberostar, Tom had a chance to make a few calls back to Washington, which seemed a world-away as his honeymoon week was winding down. The ladies seemed anxious to get the men on their way to the cockfights, so that they could have more girl time, this time hopefully without the presence of the local gendarmes.

Rather than have the Iberostar van drop them off at the gallera, Tom preferred the anonymity of a local taxi that they flagged down outside the hotel on the busy street leading to the business district of Puerto Plata. The men were getting truly adventuresome to hail a cab without the assistance of Carlos, who was going to meet them at the gallera.

Tom always traveled with his well-worn backpack slung over one shoulder to give an air of casualness and especially to have somewhere to carry his impulse purchases that Cindy so abhorred. Their driver, eager to increase his tip, proved to be garrulous to the point of being annoying until he pointed to a road heading toward the mountainous area around Puerto Plata. His description of a series of small waterfalls and rapids that could be descended by tourists seeking an unusual local thrill caught the men's attention.

When the ever-cautious David asked the lawyerly question

of when was the last time anyone was hurt in this slippery play-
ground, their driver turned toward him with the look of, 'You
Americans, relax and have some fun.' The cockfights must not
have been in his definition of fun as he mentioned that years ago
the elderly rabbi from Sosua was killed when he slipped and fatally
hit his head. This river and waterfall area are rather remote and by
the time his climbing companion returned with help, the rabbi was
dead. Tom asked the driver exactly when this accident happened
and the driver shrugged his shoulders mumbling, "Sometime after
the war."

David, as much to make conversation as anything, asked,
"Who was the rabbi's climbing partner?"

The cabbie twisted and turned in his seat as his knuckles turned
white from strangling the steering wheel. David knew when he had a
defendant on the ropes. The best strategy was to let him silently stew
until he finally broke. "Can't tell you, but very important person."

"Ludwig?" Tom interjected.

"Yes, but I didn't tell you," the cabbie reluctantly volunteered.

The cabbie came to an abrupt stop a couple blocks short of the
street to the gallera as Tom realized the cabbie was very uncomfortable deviating from his canned chamber of commerce spiel
and he didn't want anyone, especially Ludwig's people, seeing him
letting out the gringos. Tom made a mental note of the cabbie's
name, Juan Hernandez, from the faded picture ID taped to the
back of the driver's headrest.

Tom was left to silently cope with the growing uneasy feeling
in the pit of his stomach as they approached the gallera. He recognized many of the same unkempt sights on the littered streets
leading to the cockfighting arena so he was starting to feel more
at ease, at least until he'd see Ludwig again. Fr. Dennis eschewed
his roman collar, attempting to blend in with his companions. A
smiling Carlos was waiting for them at the chicken wire enclosed
ticket booth holding five tickets he said were compliments of the
owner. Tom's perfunctory offer to pay for the tickets was vigorously rebuffed by the buxomly ticket seller whom they would see

again as the roving bartender once the fights began. A smiling Fr. Dennis, watching this bouncing charade, made a mental note to confess his impure thoughts in his next confession.

As they took their seats across from where Ludwig would be sitting, Tom wanted to sit next to Carlos, who was a little more reticent with his pre-fight advice since Tom had bested Ludwig without, nay contrary, to his cautious advice. Tom promised Carlos that he wouldn't be as aggressive in his betting today since he was now a married man and had to account for his money. Tom, putting on an air of innocence, asked Carlos how the fighting cocks are trained to be so violent with an unbridled killer instinct.

Carlos cautiously scanned the stands slowly filling around them before he explained in a quiet voice that the specially bred fighting cocks first train against smaller normal chickens to increase their confidence and appetite for the bloody kill. Gradually bigger roosters, some from fighting cock rejects, are introduced into the training program before they are entered into the competitive ring. Tom nodded his understanding at Carlos' simplified training explanation before he came right to the point of asking how many trainers used small monkeys as foils in the training of the fighting cocks.

Carlos looked at the still vacant seats across from them and leaned toward Tom with his hand blocking his mouth. "The rumor is that Ludwig is again using the baby monkeys for his rooster training."

"What do you mean again?" Tom questioned.

"He was caught using baby monkeys to train the young cocks a few years ago. He was made to stop by the government, which usually doesn't care what goes on here," Carlos said.

"Are the cocks, winners and losers, tested for drugs after the fight?" Tom asked.

"These screaming spectators don't care if drugs are used or not. They don't want the government controlling their only escape from their bleak day-to-day life."

"So Ludwig could be training his roosters with helpless baby monkeys and then juicing them up for their fights so they don't feel the pain inflicted by the cock they are fighting. No wonder he usually wins and hates losing to a lucky gringo like me."

Carlos looked away pretending not to hear Tom's supposition of the reason for Ludwig's cockfighting success. The four of them at lunch, before Carlos' reluctant confession of Ludwig's shady training tactics, agreed to keep their betting under control, especially with Ludwig, to avoid another major incident. Today's cockfight visit was a chance for Fr. Dennis and David to get up to speed with Tom and Neil on this legal, yet seamier side of Dominican life. Tom was thinking that the cockfights might even be the door into Ludwig's mysterious life, where he seemed to operate by his own rules with little respect for the usual norms of society. Upon Ludwig's magisterial arrival with his same two oversized bodyguards, the fights began. Tom kept an eye on Fr. Dennis and especially on David for any signs of uncontrolled horror at the brutality being played out on the bloody dirt floor a few rows below them. Ludwig and the four gringos were mutually ignoring each other while modest bets were being exchanged around the noisy gallera before each fight.

Tom and Ludwig inadvertently made eye contact at the start of the fight before the intermission. They connected on a modest five-peso bet with Tom taking the blanco rooster and Ludwig the negro rooster. After the usual preliminary pecking and slashing it was apparent that the negro rooster was the stronger and the more aggressive of the cocks. When the exhausted blanco cock quit fighting and collapsed on the dirt floor, the referee looked at Ludwig who gave a discreet head nod that the fight should be stopped before the final kill. Tom reluctantly handed over his five-pesos to the beaming Ludwig, who looked like he had just won the Irish Sweepstakes. As the gallera was emptying for intermission, Tom slung his backpack over one shoulder because it contained a bottle of water and paper towels to use after visiting the filthy restroom or the yellow stained stucco wall where the men lined up.

Ludwig's bodyguards ran interference to the secluded back corner of the wall-less bar that few of the betting patrons could afford to patronize. After the third and last supplicant emerged back into the bright afternoon sun from his meeting with Ludwig, Tom gave the high sign to the other three that now was their time to time to visit Ludwig. Carlos mysteriously disappeared to talk with some of his buddies back in the rooster-taping corner.

The bodyguards seated beside Ludwig quickly stood up in front of him when they saw the four visitors approaching. Ludwig waved them aside and asked them to get chairs for his friends. Tom thanked Ludwig for his hospitality yesterday at his house and expressed sincere disappointment that they didn't meet his wife.

After a thoughtful pause when Ludwig cupped his hands behind his head, inadvertently flexing his ample late sixties' biceps while precariously tilting his chair backward, Tom couldn't help but stare at an old scar on the inside of his left upper arm in addition to the dark scar on his left forearm that they had noticed earlier. Strange spot to have surgery on the inside of your upper arm Tom thought, as he sensed Ludwig wondering how Tom knew that he was married. Ludwig awkwardly answered that his wife was visiting the kids in the States as she was wont to do on short notice a few times a year. He mentioned that they were expecting their first grandchild and that his wife was on a shopping spree to help furnish the nursery as only an excited grandmother could. "Your wife's the former rabbi's daughter, isn't she?" Tom asked in the most deferential tone he could muster-up.

Ludwig took an extended sip from the narrow neck of his Presidente bottle while nodding his head to answer Tom's question.

"I can't imagine a more helpless feeling, isolated at the bottom of the remote waterfall with your injured father-in-law dying in your arms." Tom watched Ludwig for any sign of emotion as perhaps he said too much, driving him back into his shell.

Finally Ludwig replied with a detached far-away look. "He wasn't my father-in-law yet, just my rabbi and my sponsor. The autopsy showed two small bumps on the side of his head, each fracturing his skull. He died of a broken neck from his slip over the waterfall. I went for help but he was dead when we got back to him."

"Two bumps on the side of his skull? Striking his head at the base of the waterfall would make only one big bump, which probably broke his neck," Tom conjectured.

Ludwig lowered his head and the bottle simultaneously without saying another word. Mercifully, the scratchy PA system broke the silence announcing that the intermission was over and the fights were resuming.

Tom lingered behind the departing group and managed to furtively slip Ludwig's beer bottle into his backpack.

Returning to his cracked faded pink bowling alley seat Tom sensed that he was being watched closely by the whole gallera for signs that he was going to get even with Ludwig for his pre-intermission five-pesos loss. However, his mind was preoccupied with what he had heard in the cordial meeting with Ludwig and he didn't have the stomach for the major betting showdown with Ludwig that the spectators were anticipating.

The final fight's two roosters were brought into the ring by their handlers and Tom noticed that Ludwig was unusually stoic as the betting commenced. Carlos whispered in his ear that the blanco cock was Ludwig's. The betting didn't appear as spirited as in previous fights so Tom got Ludwig's attention with an offered five-peso bet on the blanco cock, which Ludwig immediately raised to twenty-pesos on the negro rooster. Tom glanced at Carlos with the puzzled look of why is Ludwig betting 20 pesos against his own blanco rooster? Carlos shrugged his shoulders just as Tom signaled to Ludwig indicating that the 20 pesos bet was okay without another raise.

Carlos leaned toward Tom with the comment, "I've never seen Ludwig bet against his own rooster. At times he'll not bet when one of his roosters is fighting, but never against his rooster. Good luck."

The handlers, holding the roosters above their heads for all to see, circled the fighting pit one final time before releasing them on the dirt floor. Tom's blanco cock aggressively ran a straight line to the cowering negro cock and with a lunging slash of his sharp spur taped over its stubby dew-claw caught the neck of the unprepared negro cock. The shocked losing bettors were all screaming at the negro cock to get up as if it could hear and understand their futile exhortations.

Tom tried to get Ludwig's attention to wave off the bet but the 20 pesos were already on the way to Tom. Ludwig gave Tom a big tortured smile and a departing wave as he quickly followed his bodyguards out of the gallera. Tom and his party lingered in their seats until the gallera was nearly empty. Tom needed some answers on his feelings and observations about Ludwig and Carlos was his best place to start, so he suggested they walk to the El Arrayan outdoor bar overlooking the sparkling Puerto Plata's natural harbor that provided safe anchorage for Columbus on his new world explorations.

El Arrayan's patio provided an unobstructed view of the once proud fort guarding the entrance to the harbor's silvery water, still undiscovered by the cruise ships.

With their waiter hovering over them, Tom carefully placed his backpack on the sandy concrete beside his chair and threw Ludwig's 20 pesos on the table. "Let's all drink a 'cuba libre' using Ludwig's Brugal rum." The waiter nodded his understanding of this simple order, and he was quickly replaced at table-side by two young boys toting their well-used wooden shoe-shine boxes. Tom knew that if they didn't allow these first two shoe-shiners to do their thing, they would have no peace. All their cohorts would appear out of nowhere and pester them until they finally agreed to a shoe shine. Even Carlos allowed his dusty loafers to be polished for the first time in months. Tom gave the boys a crisp five-dollar bill to cover the ordinary quarter charge per shine. After a cacophony of 'gracias,' the gleeful boys skipped away from the table anxious to tell their buddies of their big score. Tom's generosity was as much for the hard working boys to take the money home to their struggling families as to curry the good will of Carlos for the frank conversation that Tom needed to have with him.

As an ice-breaker the round table occupants were happy to allow Fr. Dennis to expound on the deep theological and sociological meaning of the gruesome cockfights they had just attended. He was sure that the vanquished roosters went immediately to chicken heaven, but he wasn't sure of the ultimate fate of the screaming blood thirsty participants who took leave of their senses during the heat of the matches. "Wish they could show half as much excitement at church," was his doleful summation of the day's spectacle.

Outside of Fr. Dennis' obvious priesthood, Carlos wasn't aware of the occupations of his fellow Brugal tasters. David proposed a toast to Ludwig while asking Carlos how long Ludwig had been the boss at the Brugal distillery not far from where they were sipping its product.

Carlos proudly remembered that his family came to Puerto Plata from Spain before Ludwig, who started working at the distillery right away. The rumor at the time was that the Brugal Rum distillery was on the verge of closing and that Ludwig, with his family's history of owning breweries in Germany, had saved it, so that today it is the area's largest employer.

Tom's ears perked up at this background information, but he was content to let David do his lawyerly probing. Carlos seemed to recall that Ludwig once mentioned a family brewery near Berlin as early on he tried to initiate a summer Rum Fest celebration like Munich's October Fest. Ludwig became somewhat embittered at the lack of support from the local small businesses busy in a day-to-day survival mode with meager resources to devote to his new idea. Especially hurtful was the apathy, after their rabbi died in the waterfall accident while hiking with him, of his fellow Jewish immigrants toward any of his ideas that reminded them of Hitler's Germany.

These immigrants, fortunate to escape Hitler's holocaust machine through an underground railroad through Switzerland and Italy to Spain, had arrived in the Dominican Republic with barely the clothes on their backs. The Dominican government gave the refugees eighty acres to become farmers at Sosua near Puerto Plata, in spite of the fact that most of them had been city dwellers back in Europe. They literally had to scratch out a living in the fortunately fertile Dominican soil and over the years had come to prosper with dairy farms and sugar cane plantations.

Ludwig had been engaged to the rabbi's daughter at the time of the rabbi's fatal waterfall accident. The wedding was postponed a year to give everyone a chance to recover from the loss of the beloved rabbi, who had been the sponsor and early supporter of many of the immigrant families. As Ludwig's sponsor, the rabbi was intimately familiar with Ludwig's personal and family history in Germany, which Ludwig had hoped was never shared with anyone. The rabbi had a steel trap memory of the details of his immigrants' personal histories in Germany, but he keep no written notes or records because of his well-founded paranoia that his Jewish people were never totally safe from persecuting governments, even the host Dominican Republic. Thus he died as the only one who knew the details of each immigrant's unique history.

Tom could not resist asking Carlos about the rabbi's slip and fatal fall. Carlos remembered that everyone was surprised that the aging, un-athletic rabbi would attempt this strenuous activity except that he trusted and must have wanted to spend time with his future son-in-law. Carlos recalled that the rabbi had a broken pelvis and vertebrae from butt sliding down the water fall but that he died of brain hemorrhaging from a number of skull fractures on the sides of his head, possibly caused by being struck by pointed rocks. These were not consistent with a tumbling type of fall that would have caused broad depressed skull fractures. As Carlos continued to remember more details about the rabbi and his suspicious death, Tom wondered if anyone else had the same gut reaction that something was amiss in Ludwig's story from the very beginning.

The young man who was serving their table was resting at the end of the bar with his crutches leaning against the wall. Carlos called out his name, "Choque," and flashed a five-finger sign for a round of Presidente beers since their rum and cokes were finished. Each of Choque's crutches had two large cups duct-taped to it that were large enough to hold the over-sized Presidente beer bottles and Choque carried the fifth bottle against one hand rest. "It looks like he could bring six beers if he had to," Fr. Dennis said in awe.

"He has pockets and he can pinch them under his arms if he doesn't open them at the bar. I've seen him deliver ten beers without spilling a drop," Carlos proudly boasted.

"What's his name? It sounds a little unusual," Fr. Dennis questioned.

"We call him Choque, ever since his motorcycle accident that cost him a leg. The name Choque means crash."

"Is that why we see so many men on crutches?" Father wondered.

"Si, and there are more everyday. Choque's accident was typical. He tried to pass a Brugal truck on a curve and lost control of his motorcycle on loose gravel and clipped an oncoming car with his left leg. The local doctors said that the leg could probably be saved at the big hospital in Santa Domingo but Choque had no money for the helicopter trip there."

"What a shame. Wouldn't Brugal help since their truck was involved?" Father naively asked.

Carlos quickly glanced around the table and made sure that Choque was out of hearing range. "Brugal denied any responsibility for the accident and didn't want to establish a precedent by paying for Choque's medevac helicopter flight. Choque tried to get a job at Brugal after the accident and his leg was cut-off, but Ludwig told him that he didn't run a rehabilitation center. However, as a parting goodwill gesture, Ludwig gave Choque a lifetime free-pass to the cockfights, as if he would have any money to bet there."

The table sat in stunned silence thinking about the plight of their good- natured table server. Fr. Dennis wiped a tear from the corner of his eye at this cruel tale of Ludwig's totally self-absorbed narcissism. Tom was hoping against hope that Ludwig was not just a rich tycoon who had no feelings or consideration for the people and things like dead roosters around him. The question, "Was he always like this? vexed Tom probably more than what

Ludwig actually did. One thing Tom knew for sure was that he had to learn as much as he could about Ludwig before they headed home. "What about Ludwig's wife and kids?" Tom asked with a bit of agitation in his voice.

Carlos again nervously scanned the table to make sure that no one was within hearing distance. "Medical care here in the Dominican Republic has never been good enough for Ludwig. He and his wife have had surgery in Miami by Dr. Eggert who used to live and work here as one of the Jewish refugees until he moved to Florida to get more surgical training. Ludwig's children were born in Miami, so they are US citizens."

Tom remembered that a pill bottle in the medicine cabinet had the name of a Miami hospital pharmacy on it. His thoughts were interrupted as Carlos continued.

"We hardly ever see Naomi here in Puerto Plata anymore. She has full-time help that even does her shopping for her. Occasionally, she attends the small synagogue in Sosua and seems to have some friends there, although many have died or emigrated back to Europe or to new homes in America. When her children were at Aiglion boarding school in Switzerland, she spent a lot of time visiting them. When they went to college in America, she was always over there. We don't consider Ludwig and his family Dominicans even though they have lived here a long time and they gave their kids Dominican sounding names, Bernardo and Susana."

"Makes you wonder what country they really consider home and what passports they carry," the lawyer David commented.

"Now you know why Ludwig always is surrounded by security. He is still viewed as a wealthy outsider, making a lot of money that some of our own people resent and could be making themselves."

XIII

Tom was surprised at Carlos' frankness and he didn't want to give Carlos the impression that he was pumping him for information on Ludwig, so he asked Carlos about his own family.

Carlos's face brightened, relieved of the strain and tension from talking about Ludwig, as he proudly started to tell his four gringo friends about his three children. His oldest son was a doctor in Madrid, probably never to return home to practice after seeing the glories of Spain. His daughter was a school teacher in the capital of Santo Domingo, about two hours away. The youngest son was studying to be a priest in the seminary at San Juan, Puerto Rico.

Fr. Dennis gave Carlos an exuberant high-five at this revelation and was pleased to hear that he would be ordained a priest in only two more years. Fr. Dennis told Carlos that he would be greatly honored to be invited to his son's ordination.

Carlos' smile was mitigated by his comment that his wife was anxious for mucho grand children and the priesthood wouldn't help that. Fortunately, her job as supervisor of the large cleaning and maid staff at the Iberostar resort kept her too busy to obsess over the grandchild issue.

Fr. Dennis' comment, with a tinge of wishful thinking, "Priests soon might be able to get married," brought negative head shakes all around the table.

Carlos mentioned how he has had a good life especially compared to his parents who came here from Madrid at the start of World War II. His father had been the janitor of a large Jewish synagogue and his mother had been a servant for wealthy families in Madrid, so the family had a good life in Spain before coming to the Dominican Republic.

Tom's question, "So why did they move to a new life here that was less certain than their life in Spain?" brought a thoughtful pause from Carlos.

Carlos again looked around to see that no one was within earshot of the table. "The synagogue sent my dad and mom here with the old rabbi as advance people for the Jewish settlers who were being allowed to immigrate to the Dominican Republic, which was the only Western country that would accept Jews as policies started to change in Germany and in their conquered countries. The synagogue paid my dad and mother's expenses and kept my dad on their payroll for two years after he moved here so he could continue to help the immigrant Jewish families. My parents loved it here, away from the war in Europe."

"Did your dad ever talk about the backgrounds of the Jews who came here?" Tom asked.

"He didn't talk much about them because he didn't know much about their backgrounds when they first arrived. Only the rabbi knew the immigrants' backgrounds and he didn't tell that to anyone. Once their dairy farms and sugar cane plantations started becoming prosperous, their stories started to emerge. Most of the immigrants, except Ludwig, were poor when they arrived, but they have all done well as you can see by their farms and plantations at Sosua where they settled."

"You say Ludwig had money when he got here, so he didn't work?" Tom asked.

"All the Jewish immigrants had to work from the first day that they arrived, except Ludwig. The rabbi kept telling everyone that they were trying to get him a job at the Brugal plant because of his family's experience with breweries back in Germany. The word was that Ludwig supported the rabbi's family when he first lived with them. Of course that's how he met Naomi, who became his wife after the rabbi died. The rabbi was opposed to his daughter marrying Ludwig so soon after he got here because of something that he knew about Ludwig."

"What was that?" Gleason asked.

"I don't know. My father seemed to know but he never told us."

"I'm really curious how the Jews escaped out of Germany and got all the way over here to the Dominican Republic," Tom said

"Each family of refugees had a different escape saga to relate. Like I said, many only recently have started to talk about their journey as they are finally feeling secure here. They all came through the synagogue in Madrid where my dad worked. How they got to Madrid from all over Europe: Germany, Poland, Ukraine, France, and other countries is the true miracle of this small diaspora. I remember someone mentioning that Ludwig came to Madrid from Rome and maybe Switzerland."

"Did your father keep any notes about the refugees and their stories?" Tom asked.

"He said that he was told by the chief rabbi in Madrid not to keep written notes or pictures in case they fell into the hands of the Nazis. However, as he got older, to help him remember the people he still felt responsible for, he started to keep a shoebox of pictures and other papers about the refugees."

"Do you still have the shoebox?" Tom asked.

Carlos looked down to avoid making eye contact with the four gringos. Tom nervously tapped his finger-tips on the table as Carlos twisted and squirmed in his chair until he answered quietly, "I still have my father's shoebox, but I don't look at it much for fear of what it might contain."

"About Ludwig?"

Carlos nodded. Tom thought he had nothing to lose, so he asked, "Can I see it before I leave?"

"I'll bring it tomorrow. Most of the material is in Spanish."

Neil jumped to Tom's aid, "I read Spanish pretty well, but don't ask me to speak it."

Tom pushed his chair away from the table and stood up. "The ladies will be waiting for us back at the hotel to eat dinner." When Carlos stepped to the curb to hail a taxi for the four of them back to the hotel, Tom wrapped a napkin around Carlos' Presidente beer bottle so as not to smudge Carlos' fingerprints and to prevent it from clinking against Ludwig's bottle. Then he slipped it into his backpack. He left a 20 pesos bill on the table for Choque to bet at the cockfights—small chance of that he smiled to himself since Ludwig owned the gallera and went to every cockfighting match.

Back at the Iberostar for dinner, Fr. Dennis concluded his dinner blessing with the hope that everyone connected with the dehumanizing cockfighting business would seek more humane jobs that would allow them to respect all forms of life, even the lowly chickens, which he hoped were not on their dinner plates tonight.

The wives were excited to report on their shopping trip to the infamous Orange Mall on the beach. Tom was lost in thought as the women passed around their Larimar and Amber jewelry pieces for all to admire. He wondered what secrets the shoebox would reveal when Carlos brought it the next day.

XIV

Carlos stopped by Tom's breakfast table and whispered that he would like to bring the shoebox to his room where Tom could keep it overnight. Tom agreed that he would be back to his room in an hour and waiting for him. Neil was volunteered to help since he could read Spanish, and David said that it sounded like they might need a lawyer. Fr. Dennis gladly chimed in that he would enjoy a leisurely day at the beach with the ladies.

Waiting in Tom's room, the men commiserated that they hated to spend a whole day cooped-up looking at stuff when they didn't know what they were looking for. Carlos's gentle knock brought Tom to immediately open the door. "Please lock the shoebox in your suitcase when you leave your room so the maid doesn't see it," was Carlos' only communication as he quickly took the shoebox out of a worn shopping bag and handed it to Tom without going into the room.

Tom turned the inside lock on the door to thwart a maid's surprise entry. The three of them pulled up chairs around the end of the bed as Tom gently spread out the yellowing contents of the box. Neil was elected to do a quick scan of each piece and to sort them into three piles: 1—not pertinent to Ludwig; 2—possibly pertinent to Ludwig; 3—definitely pertinent to Ludwig. Pile 1 grew rapidly as Neil quickly filtered out birth, wedding and death notices of the small Jewish community at Sosua. Pile 3 also grew rapidly with material that directly mentioned Ludwig such as notes and yellowing newspaper articles about him managing the Brugal Rum factory and owning the cockfighting gallera.

Pile 2 contained the most intriguing information that caused the three of them to wonder why Carlos' father had saved this mostly anonymous information in the form of his own hand-written notes or a few letters in their original envelopes from Europe, mainly Germany and Spain, and Argentina. David held up three empty envelopes addressed to L.W. at the Brugal Rum Factory, that only had return addresses of DM, 88, Argentina. "Wonder what the contents of these envelopes was?" David questioned, "And how did Carlos's father come into possession of them?"

Once this preliminary sorting was done, Tom tipped back in his chair and wondered aloud, "There's some strange stuff here, especially since we don't know what the hell we're even looking for."

Neil did a quick read through of the items in pile 2 with his CIA antenna fully extended and concluded that there seemed to be a common thread connecting many of these notes and letters without any names mentioned. He admitted that his Spanish skills were not as fluent as his wife's, Joanne's, and that they should have her look at them. Tom immediately squashed that idea so as not to incur the wrath of his new bride for working while on their honeymoon.

Neil dug his miniature camera out of his Bermuda short's pocket and waved it over pile 2 like he was taking a picture of an enemy's classified material. "Tom, our choices are to spend the final days of your honeymoon holed-up in your room trying to decipher this material, or we could copy it for analysis by our experts at Langley."

"That's an easy choice," Tom answered. "Take your pictures so we can join our wives at the beach."

"Wait just a minute," David jumped in. "It is illegal to copy this material without the owner's permission. I don't want to go to a Dominican jail."

Tom threw his hands up in the air. "David! Who asked your legal opinion? Besides you just said it was junk. Neil, just take pictures of piles 2 and 3 so we can join the wives and Fr. Dennis at the beach. I'll tell Carlos what we did."

After the pertinent pictures were taken, Tom shuffled and mixed up the three piles on the bed before putting everything, except for one of the three envelopes from South America back into the shoebox. Rather than locking-up the musty box in Cindy's suitcase with her jewels and nicer clothes, he called Carlos to see if he would come to get the box. David and Neil left to change into their beach attire while Tom waited for Carlos to retrieve the shoebox. Carlos had the same old shopping bag when he arrived. This time Tom motioned for him to come into the room so he could shut and lock the door. "Why'd your father save this box full of stuff? Some of it is quite old."

"I think it was a remembrance of his friends that he helped. I haven't looked at it since he died years ago. I guess that I saved it because of his hand written notes, which are the only samples of his hand-writing that I have. He continued to help many of the Jewish immigrants as a sort of handyman until he died. They trusted him with many of their personal problems and we were invited to many of their birthday parties, bar mitzvahs and weddings."

"Your father sounds like a wonderful person."

"He was, and I have always tried to make him proud of me," Carlos said.

"Carlos, I would like to ask you to continue saving your dad's box. Does anyone else know that you have it?"

"Only my wife. Every time she cleans the house, she wants to throw it out."

"Don't let her do that. There are too many memories of your father in it." Tom thought it best not to tell Carlos of their photographing some of the box's contents so as not to alarm him that there might be something valuable beyond his father's memories.

Tom's arrival at the beach was greeted by a robust chorus of, 'For He's A Jolly Good Fellow.' intoned by the ever-mischievous Fr. Dennis.

Tom snuggled on his beach towel beside his grinning bride. "Can you now relax and enjoy the final days of our honeymoon?" she pleaded.

He didn't want to risk being labeled a liar, either now or at a later date, so he let his kiss on Cindy's reddening cheek be his answer. He knew that he needed the quiet beach time to sort out the peripheral matters that were impinging on his and for sure his wife's enjoyment of the final days of their honeymoon.

A round of drinks would help everyone relax he thought so he summoned the beach waiter to take their refreshment orders. He paid with a crisp one hundred dollar bill and the waiter gave Tom a worn fifty-dollar bill as part of his change. Tom examined it and passed it around the group with the question, "What do you think?"

Cindy, not knowing what Tom was referring to elbowed him in the ribs as a matter of principle. "Do you think that any of us really care about this crumpled old fifty?"

"Well, maybe we should all care about it since it's probably counterfeit just like the fifty that I won from Ludwig at the cock-fight and the one that I got back as change at the Brugal gift shop." Tom didn't want to risk Cindy's renewed wrath by explaining that the Secret Service was established after the Civil War to preserve the integrity of the Union money supply and that this mandate was still an important part of Secret Service work in addition to its better known job of protecting the President. Tom pocketed this bogus beach fifty to bring back to his office in D.C. along with the two other fifties from the cockfight and the Brugal gift shop.

Tom was already planning his presentation of the suspected counterfeit bills to his boss as soon as he got back to Washington. Tom was not at liberty to tell his friends in the wedding party that his boss, on the day before he left for the wedding, had recommended him for transfer to the Presidential Protective

Division—PPD—of the Secret Service. He questioned the need to immediately tell Cindy, preoccupied as she was with their wedding plans. However, he figured it better to tell her now than presenting it as a fait accompli at a later date, so he casually had worked it into their conversation on the flight down. Her reaction was supportive, as he knew it would be, but she passed it off with the question of, "How long will it be before you know if you're chosen for this new job?"

Tom explained that there were no guaranties that he would be accepted into the highly coveted PPD of the Secret Service just because he was recommended for it. The PPD had the highest profile of any of the divisions of the Secret Service within the Department of the Treasury because of its mandate to protect our leaders of government, especially the president. It was considered an honor to be recommended for this promotion, even though the burnout rate of agents assigned there was high after a few years because of the 24/7 pressure of protecting the president.

Tom was content to continue in his present job of working for the Secret Service in its revenue division and the turning over of the counterfeit bills from his Dominican honeymoon was right in keeping with his job. However, he was reluctant to tell Cindy how much he would like an appointment to the PPD as it would mean that he would not be home as much as his current 8 to 5 job allowed.

XV

The first day back to work after a vacation can often be a letdown. It was especially so for Tom, since his wedding and honeymoon were so compressed into an intense week that was already morphing into a series of blurred memories. However, Tom was still invigorated as he carried his briefcase into his Treasury building office well before his normal 8 AM starting time. He had his secretary request an emergency appointment with his boss and he was given a time just before the noon lunch break.

As he sorted through his week's worth of mail and phone messages, he started to think that maybe he should not have called it an emergency meeting with his boss. Would his boss consider it a little presumptuous of an up-and-coming agent to essentially demand an immediate appointment as the "emergency" request connoted? 'Too late to take it back,' Tom thought to himself as he arranged the evidence he wanted to show him at the noon meeting.

The three $50.00 bills that Tom suspected to be counterfeit would be easy to explain and they could be verified as legal or counterfeit very quickly. The two Presidente beer bottles, still in their protective baggies, would take more explanation.

At the appointed time he took the elevator upstairs to his boss's corner office overlooking the White House. When the secretary motioned for him to go in, he crossed the large room toward his boss, George seated behind his cluttered desk. "Had a working honeymoon, sir," Tom said, as he struggled to find a clear place to place the evidence.

"Couldn't have been all work! You at least had a couple beers," George replied, spotting the two Presidente bottles.

"I also picked up some funny money," Tom said as he placed the three fifty dollars on the desk in front of George.

George did what everyone does when suspicious of a large denomination bill: he held each one up to the bright overhead fluorescent light. "Not too bad a match for the real thing. However, all three have the same serial number, so that's pretty conclusive. Where did you get them?"

"They are souvenirs from my wedding and honeymoon in the Dominican Republic. The most crumpled-up one came from our resort's beach bar and the other two came from the person who drank the Presidente beer in bottle One. Bottle Two has the fingerprints of someone I want to check out as a possible snitch in getting to know the owner of the prints on bottle one."

Somewhat confused, George tilted back in his chair, deep in thought behind closed eyes to block out the bright ceiling lights. "Gleason, is this your way of getting the Treasury Department to reimburse you one-hundred-fifty bucks of your honeymoon money?"

Tom's face turned even redder than his final beach day's sunburn. When he saw the corners of George's mouth slightly elevate creating a smile not quite reaching his flickering eyes, he dared to say, "Not a bad idea, chief. I'll be sure to include the one-fifty in my expense account."

Tom noticed the large institutional clock behind his boss's desk creeping up on noon so he figured that he'd better get to the point. Without going into the graphic details of the cockfights and the ladies' encounter with Ludwig's beach law, Tom tried to objectively paint a picture of Ludwig as he knew him. Tom thought it more than coincidental that two of the bogus fifty-dollar bills could be traced back to Ludwig either at the cockfight or at his

Brugal company's gift store. The crumpled beach fifty-dollar bill could be just a random bill that was floating around the Dominican financial system unless Ludwig had some inside connection to an Iberostar's money laundering scheme.

They agreed that they needed to send the three bills to their crime lab to try to determine their origin and to search for any latent fingerprints that might match anyone in their file of known counterfeiters. Counterfeit bills can have a long life of their own in third world countries as their unsophisticated banking systems often seem happy to have any form of United States dollars in circulation. Of course, the hardship of accepting counterfeit falls on the small shop owners or service people like cab drivers who get stuck with these worthless bills if their local bank won't accept them.

The two wrapped and bagged green Presidente bottles caught George's attention more than the counterfeit bills that fall under his purview as head of the Secret Service. Gleason explained how the two bottles could be connected as the fingerprints of Carlos were on the bottle labeled number Two, and he seemed to have a relationship with Ludwig whose fingerprints were on bottle number One. Carlos, since he worked for the Iberostar Resort could be responsible for introducing the counterfeit bills into the resort's money supply. Gleason felt that his three phony bills could be just the tip of the iceberg in the sweltering Dominican Republic and the bottom line was that Gleason just wanted to know the real identity of Ludwig and Carlos and if they had criminal records.

Unless evidence was tagged, 'Urgent - Top Secret,' the intake clerk at the Department of Treasury's criminal lab assigned any submitted evidence a routine number and placed in a line to be gotten to when it was gotten to. In the meantime Gleason was able to do some background checking on his own. Most counterfeiting, especially outside the United States, is a product of small time criminals who have probably been doing it their whole lives, having learned the craft from a relative or friend.

The advent of high quality color copy machines has put a lot of the old-fashioned engravers in the unemployment lines.

The three fifty-dollar bills were determined to be counterfeit by the naked eye, especially with the same serial number. An added advantage is that the lab could detect mistakes invisible to the naked eye that serve as fingerprints on each bill and possibly give a clue as to their country of origin. All three of the bills seemed to have been crimped or folded at one time into a long rectangle, one third of their width, to possibly fit into a zippered money belt. It would be easier to trace these bills if they were determined to be from the same counterfeiting operation. The Secret Service often would not get much cooperation from third world countries in tracking down counterfeiters because these countries felt that US dollars—real or counterfeit—circulating in their economies was a good thing. If all the counterfeit bills were rounded up and taken out of circulation in some of these small, impoverished countries, their economies would take a serious blow.

One week later Gleason had a phone message to contact his boss, George, about an appointment as soon as possible, which Gleason knew meant right now. While he waited in George's anteroom, he wondered if the lab analyses of the fifty-dollar bills and the two Presidente beer bottles were back this soon. His own cursory background checks of Ludwig and Carlos were unproductive so he was anticipating any help that the lab tests could provide.

"Shut the door, Gleason, and have a seat," George barked in a harsher tone than he really meant. "I have two items to talk about: one good and one bad. How do you want them?"

Gleason shrugged his shoulders leaving it up to George to decide how he wanted to proceed.

"Okay, the bad news is that your application to become part of the Presidential Protective Division has been put on a six-month hold because of the damn federal freeze on any new hiring. Looks like you'll be stuck working with me for a few more months," George said with a big smile.

"Hey, Boss, that could be the good news."

"You might be right, based on these criminal lab results that I have. However, the good news is that I'm assigning you to work full-time on this case. You might even get a chance to return to the Dominican Republic for a second honeymoon. Hopefully, this time non-working."

The Treasury lab officially confirmed that the three fifty-dollar bills were counterfeit and came from a common printing source based on the same discrepancies found in all the bills. However, the paper was different on all three bills. The three papers were high quality paper, probably from Europe, that was a close match to the real paper of authentic US bills. The counterfeiters probably bought paper from three different sources to lessen the risk inherent in placing one large order that could draw attention to their purchase of this expensive specialty paper. This split paper purchasing showed the sophistication of these counterfeiters who must have been aware of the Secret Service breaking previous counterfeiting rings by tracing the paper backward to its point of sale.

The fact that the counterfeit bills were of the fifty-dollar denomination and not the more easily passed twenty-dollar or lesser denomination bills led George and Gleason to believe that the counterfeiters were getting bolder and impatient to achieve a bigger payoff. The bills could have been printed anywhere in the world and then a distribution network established using shovers to get the bills into circulation.

None of the same counterfeit bills had surfaced anywhere else, so George and Gleason decided to take a "wait and see" posture before getting overly aggressive about the three bills Gleason brought back from the Dominican Republic. He explained to his boss that if Ludwig were connected with this counterfeiting operation, he most certainly was not just a lowly shover passing out a few bogus bills. He would be involved in the bigger picture, knowing where the bills were printed and the distribution network.

George handed the two-page lab reports of bottle one and bottle two to Gleason, who took a few minutes to read them before looking up. "Typical lab report posing as many questions as answers."

"Hell, Gleason, you gave them two beer bottles from a

thousand miles away that had been handled by who knows how many people, so naturally there are multiple fingerprints on each bottle. What do you expect of the lab?"

"I guess that we must assume that the prints that we are interested in are the most numerous on the bottles since the drinker would have picked up the bottle many times. Can we ask the lab to focus in on these most numerous prints from each bottle and come up with a possible identity?"

"The lab will do whatever I ask, but it'll take a while since they'll have to go to international fingerprint sources. I'll contact you when I hear back from them."

XVI

While he was waiting to hear back from the lab, Gleason enlisted the help of his best man, Neil, to see if the pictures that they had taken of the contents of Carlos's box of memorabilia had been analyzed by the CIA. Neil explained to Gleason that his material was of very low priority since there was no obvious threat to national security, but nevertheless, it was in the CIA's pipeline, probably assigned to a junior analyst or even an intern. Neil commented that this might get them a more thorough analysis than if a senior analyst just skimmed through it versus the younger person who would be careful not to miss anything that might impact a future job with the agency.

Neil told Gleason that the one purloined envelope addressed to L.W. at the Brugal Rum Factory at Puerto Plata with the return address in Argentina, DM, 88 was very interesting. The fragmentary Argentina address was a verified address for known Nazi sympathizers and possibly a safe house for Nazi war criminals after the Second World War. Rumor had it that the notorious concentration camp doctor, Dr. Josef Mengele, spent time at that address. The number 88 was used among Nazi sympathizer as a code for Heil Hitler since H is the eighth letter of the alphabet.

The letter was obviously between like-minded individuals so

Gleason and Neil were confounded by the contradiction of why anyone in the small Dominican Jewish community would be corresponding with their hated oppressors hiding out in Argentina after the war. Neil offered to have the handwriting on the envelope analyzed for a possible match with known Nazis, including Mengele, who could have lived in Argentina.

Gleason and Neil decided that they must proceed with caution, being mindful of the role that Carlos and his father played in helping to settle the Jewish community in the Dominican Republic. Neil offered to try to have an answer on the handwriting analysis by the time Gleason met with his boss on the fingerprints on the bottles.

Gleason had written himself a note to help remember the date on the Disney World photo of Ludwig's family hanging on the living room wall during their tour of the ocean-side mansion. Until Gleason was put through to a supervisor at Disney World's Orlando office, he was getting nowhere with the initial phone screeners who claimed that they could not divulge the name of the family in the photo.

Once the supervisor became convinced of the veracity of Gleason's identity and the importance of his request, she agreed to check into his request, stating that she would need a day or two to track down all the photos taken that day. Gleason explained to her that the picture was taken on Main Street with the front of Cinderella's castle in the background, so that she could immediately eliminate all the other photos taken that day by the roaming Disney photographers.

While waiting to hear back from Disney on the photo information, Gleason called the pharmacy in Miami that had filled the eye-drop prescription that Gleason had seen and photographed in Ludwig's medicine cabinet. Not surprisingly Gleason was totally denied any personal information by the pharmacy clerk who quoted all the federal and state laws protecting patient's privacy. Gleason's persistent questioning did at least establish that this prescription was indeed filled at this pharmacy. As a veteran of many of these cat and mouse investigations Gleason knew that he would have to get the local Treasury field office involved where court orders could be obtained to expedite the investigations. Miami was definitely on his travel radar screen along with Disney World at Orlando.

Gleason was delighted to receive the message from Neil that they should get together as soon as possible to go over the report from the CIA analyst on their photographs of the documents from Carlos's musty shoebox.

Their attention was immediately drawn to item CIA numbered, 1944 – 9, which was a letter from a rabbi in Spain addressed to the rabbi in the Dominican Republic stating, 'The enclosed check for 5,000 pesos is for any expenses connected with the package arriving on the next freighter from Spain. The suspicious package and this check were sent by wealthy family members through their Swiss bankers. The family needs the package safeguarded indefinitely with you in the Dominican Republic. You will need to hold the package long after the war even though it will be wanted back in Germany.'

"Sure would be nice to know what was in the package," Neil wondered.

"I don't think anything was in the package," Gleason quickly answered. "The package was a person arriving on the passenger freighter. A suspicious person no less!"

"Are you thinking of the same person that I am? Herr Ludwig Walther," Neil said, answering his own question.

The two sleuths thought it highly unusual that this sponsoring rabbi in Madrid would cast dispersions on this referred refugee, calling him a suspicious package, when he was about to be accepted by the rabbi in the Dominican Republic. It was agreed that they needed to verify when Walther actually arrived in the DR and then begin the process of retracing Ludwig Walther's steps back into Germany.

Even if the rabbi in Spain was deceased, as they knew that the first rabbi in the DR was, there was an address for the Synagogue in Madrid where there might be records of refugees who were resettled. They decided that is was best not to contact the rabbi and the synagogue at Sosua so as not to alert Ludwig that they were looking into his background.

Back in his office Gleason added this CIA material to his growing file on Ludwig Walther. 'Strange,' he thought, 'that the file on the uncharged Walther was growing thicker than many of his closed files on bank robbers and counterfeiters.'

With that uncertainty about Walther in mind, Gleason needed to seek the direction of his boss, even though he had to steel himself for a possible rejection of continuing to pursue the case when he entered the boss's office. "Where the hell is this investigation of this Ludwig Walther going? I thought that we were dealing with a petty counterfeiting case down in the Caribbean," his boss George barked.

"I wish I knew myself where this will lead us, sir. I have that cop's intuition that things with Ludwig aren't what they appear," Gleason replied.

"Okay, Gleason since your career here is in limbo waiting for your transfer to the presidential protection division, have at it chasing down any suspicious leads on Walther beyond the counterfeiting issue. Just don't embarrass me or the department as I'm too young to be retired."

"Thank you, sir. I'll keep you informed."

As Gleason was headed back to his office, a moment of panic hit him as he realized that he would have a harder sell convincing his wife that this side-track of his secure and comfortable Department of Treasury career was in their best interest. So he left a phone message at home for Cindy, knowing that she was still at work, asking if they could go to Old Ebbitt's Grill tonight to celebrate their one-month wedding anniversary and to discuss a new job opportunity for him. Hopefully, this message would peak Cindy's interest in his rather nebulous future investigation.

Their table at Old Ebbitt's Grill was the same table where Tom had proposed to Cindy a year and a half earlier. He hoped that this rather secluded table tucked behind a vine covered pillar would not let him down in this second important request he had to make of Cindy. He felt that this special table was second only to the totally secluded and private White House table, where the White House Secret Service agents could unwind from their stress-filled days of protecting the president.

Tom knew that his new bride appreciated the safety and certainty of his current low profile Secret Service job and had half-heartedly approved his request for a transfer to the Presidential Protective Division because she knew how much it meant to him, and there was a good chance that it would never come to fruition. This current open-ended career sidetrack was going to be ticklish to present to Cindy, but probably no more so than their first date. Cindy was the only woman in a Cosmology philosophy class filled with seminarians studying for the Catholic priesthood. She needed this required class, as did the seminarians, for their degrees in philosophy.

She had been surprised when Tom, in full priestly black cassock and Roman collar, approached her after a lecture one day and asked if she had time to get a coke. He survived the nervousness of this bold first date and the rest was history leading to today's one month anniversary dinner celebration with an ulterior purpose.

After receiving her Ph.D., Cindy was now starting her teaching career in the Philosophy Department at Catholic University where she and Tom had met. She liked the way the pieces of their present working lives fit together so Tom's mention that he might have to make trips back to the Dominican Republic and to Florida to follow-up on the counterfeiting investigation caught her by surprise. He updated her on the fact that the fifty-dollar bills that he brought back from their honeymoon were indeed counterfeit and that the hated—at least by the women—Ludwig was the prime suspect in this investigation.

Tom's assurance that this was only a temporary reassignment until his new White House assignment happened softened her so he was relieved when she said she needed to get home to prepare tomorrow's lecture and grade papers.

XVII

The Secret Service, the FBI, the CIA and most other federal agencies are good at record keeping and building files to be used as evidence to bolster their cases of how busy and essential their roles are. Getting all the agencies to share their information and to work together is the challenge, especially at the field agent level.

On his flight to Orlando, Gleason had the quiet time he needed to review a thick file listing all the counterfeit bills that were confiscated in the continental United States during the past 3 years. He was flipping through the fifty-dollar bill section of the file when he was stopped cold by the subtitle of: Florida, Disney World. He found a listing of four fifty-dollar bills that were passed about the same date as was on the photo that he was flying to Orlando to investigate.

Getting in to see the proper person, the CEO at Disney World, proved to be as formidable as trying to see the President of the United States. However, the ever-image conscious Disney World was not about to risk the wrath of the powerful Department of Treasury over the simple request of the identity of a family in an old photo.

Gleason added a local Secret Service agent and a FBI agent to his team before meeting with the Disney World CEO. The CEO was prepared for the meeting with ten pictures of families with four people taken from the picture spot on Main Street with Cinderella's castle in the background that Gleason had described. Without hesitation Gleason fingered the picture of Ludwig and his family. "What do your records show about this family?"

The CEO tilted back in his chair, stroking his chin, before answering Gleason's door-opening question. "I should be asking you the same question, Mr. Gleason."

"Sorry, I asked first," Gleason replied in an adolescent game of chicken.

The CEO started flipping through a folder of pages that Gleason could see was the date in question. He circled with a red pencil the two lines he was looking for and pushed it across his desk for Gleason to examine.

Gleason smiled at reading the name, Ludwig Walther family, but the home address section listed Germany and the method of payment for the forty dollar photo charge was cash. It was noted that the photos would be picked up with no mailing address supplied. Gleason's mind was swirling about how much to divulge to the CEO, but he quickly realized that he had the CEO on his side so he laid out the counterfeiting scenario: four identical fifty-dollar bills were recovered from Disney World about the time of the photo and the Treasury Department had similar counterfeit bills which were passed at other locations at approximately the same time.

The CEO stood up and paced nervously behind his desk, pausing to look out his window at Cinderella's castle starting to awaken with the early rush of excited morning visitors.

Gleason knew that this powerful CEO wasn't worried about the two hundred dollars that Disney World had to absorb by accepting this counterfeit money so he waited for him to speak.

Finally, the CEO stopped pacing and stood behind his chair, steadying himself on its back. "This case doesn't make sense. If someone from Germany exchanged Germany money for American money what are the chances of him being given four identical counterfeit bills at a bank or reputable airport money exchange?"

"Zero," Gleason answered.

The CEO picked up the picture and quickly scanned it before handing it to Gleason. "Look at their clothes. Their American shoes are a dead-giveaway, as Europeans wear different shoes than we do. The woman's clothes are rather upscale for a day at the park, perhaps from a fancy New York designer. The kids' clothes could be from any Ralph Lauren Polo store. The father in his aviator sunglasses is more obscure in the shadows."

"Your observations are right-on," Gleason commented. "When you retire from Disney, we'll have a job for you."

The four of them continued to brainstorm on ways to learn more about this unknown—except to Gleason - counterfeiting family. Gleason was interested in getting credit card information on Ludwig to help shed light on his true identity and activities outside the Dominican Republic. The CEO flipping through another report from this same time frame announced that a counterfeit bill had been processed from the Polynesian Resorts' gift shop the day after the photo was taken.

Gleason asked how much trouble it would be to check all parties of four arriving and departing the Polynesian hotel for a few days on either side of the photo day if the name of Walther was not on their guest list.

"It'll take a while," the CEO answered as he handed out Magic Kingdom day-passes for the agents with the caveat, "Stay close in case the staff comes up with a quick answer to our problem."

To kill time while the hotel search for the party of four was ongoing, Gleason wanted to go inside the Magic Kingdom and locate the Kodak picture spot where Ludwig's family picture had been taken with Cinderella's castle in the background.

Once they found the spot that was clearly marked with the Kodak Picture Spot sign, they were approached by an attractive young lady whose nametag said, 'Katy from Chicago', with an expensive camera dangling from its neck-strap. All smiles, she offered to take their picture.

Before Gleason consented to have their photo taken, he showed Katy the photo of Ludwig's family and asked if she had taken it. She looked at the date and said that she could have as she started working December 1 and the photo was dated December 22, last year. Shaking her head, she handed the photo back to Gleason. "It's not a very good picture since you can hardly make-out the father hiding in the shadow."

The four men had a few laughs as Katy tried to position them for the best shot of these middle-age fun seekers. Just when she thought that she had them properly positioned, Gleason took a step backward to simulate Ludwig's position in his picture.

"Sir, please move back where you were," Katy gently chided before taking the picture. "Now I remember. That's exactly what that man in your picture did. Except he wouldn't move back, so I just took the picture as bad as it is."

Gleason couldn't walk the few feet to Katy fast enough. He asked if she remembered anything else about that day. Gleason's photo reenactment of Ludwig's behavior flipped a switch in Katy's memory as she related how the man appeared upset at having the picture taken in the first place and that he quickly walked over to a couple who they appeared to be with. She noticed the unhappy man loosen his belt, take out a bill, and bring it to her to pay for the forty-dollar photo. However, he told her to keep the change, a rather large ten-dollar tip. Also she recalled that the fifty-dollar bill was very creased because it had been folded in the man's money belt and that her offer to take a picture of the six of them met with an angry rebuff, "No way," from the man in the picture. She thought that it would have been a cute picture as the couple was wearing German clothing, brightly embroidered vests and the man sporting a hat with a feather and little medals. Her offer to take a picture of just the two foreign visitors was declined with a pleasant, 'Nein danke' from the woman.

Katy explained how to get their picture at the Kodak store on Main Street. Gleason asked for Katy's Disney employee number that would allow them to reach her again if needed. The four men sat down for an ice cream cone on bustling Main Street before the big parade started. Gleason felt strongly that they should get this new information about the foreign couple to the CEO, whereas his bureaucratic cohorts didn't think it was important enough to interrupt their fun day in the park. Partly finished with his vanilla cone, Gleason announced that he was returning to the CEO's office so the other three could enjoy their free-day in the park.

The fact that Gleason was immediately escorted into the CEO's elegant inner sanctum got his heart racing. Hopefully there was a break-through in tracking down Ludwig's identity while he was visiting Disney World. This optimism was quickly changed when the CEO somberly pointed to the chair across from his desk.

"No luck finding the Walther party of four, with two adult kids, staying at the Polynesian at the time the photograph was taken."

"Speaking of luck, we had a major stoke of it at the Kodak Photo-spot where the same girl photographer was today," Gleason said. "After I showed her the family picture, she remembered taking it."

""We try to hire smart people here at Disney World, but this is ridiculous—remembering this family nearly a year later. What'd she remember?"

"The man in the photo backed into the shadow and he refused to move back so she took the picture as we see it. She recalled that they were with another couple, who appeared to be from Europe based on their clothes and their talk. The man in the picture paid her with a fifty-dollar bill that he removed from his money belt. I got your photographer's employee ID number so we can contact her."

"What country did she say the other couple was from?"

"She thought Germany."

The CEO punched his intercom button and told his secretary to notify those working on the Polynesian occupancy records to look for anyone registered from Germany. This gave Gleason time to think and remember that his Department of Treasury's lab report had noted that all of the fifty-dollar bills related to this case had prominent crease marks where the bills could have been folded lengthwise to fit in a money belt. He was reconstructing the photographer's comments when the desk-phone rang. The CEO nodded his head and told the caller to bring a copy of this registration to him immediately.

Hanging up the phone, he looked at Gleason. "We have a family of six from Germany, registered in three adjoining rooms. The name Walther is not found on any of the forms." He explained that the name Walther would not have to be on the room registration form if they were not paying for the room.

The secretary brought in two copies of the registration form under the name Schanz from Berlin that Gleason and the CEO studied. Ages were listed for the occupants of one room, male 21 and female 19 as if they were applying for a family plan. Six two-day admission tickets to the Disney parks also were charged to the room.

"Isn't it required that you have names for everyone staying in separate rooms?" Gleason asked.

" We prefer it that way so we can contact people in an emergency. But, we don't require it when someone else in the party is paying for all the rooms. What's the deal where the address of the person making the reservation is listed in the Dominican Republic and the person paying the bill is the German name?"

"The Dominican Republic is the home of the party of four in the picture so Ludwig must have made the reservation under the name of Konrad Schanz. I see phone calls were made from the rooms. I need you to retrieve the numbers called as well as the credit card information," Gleason said with no hesitation in his voice.

The CEO starred at the registration form until he finally said, "Our company policy calls for the immediate dismissal of anyone releasing confidential credit card information and also the phone calls would certainly fall into that same category."

Gleason was prepared for this legal technicality so he removed a federal court order from his briefcase regarding the identity of the party in the photography. "This should take you off the hook," he said as he handed the court order to the CEO.

"This must be a big case," the CEO said. "It will still take us a few days to get the phone numbers from the phone company as well as the credit card information."

"Any time the integrity of our money supply is attacked by counterfeiting we react strongly," Gleason said, trying to cover-up his bigger concerns about Ludwig.

Gleason was relieved to escape the white-gloved grasp of the Mouse Family at Disney World so he could pursue other avenues of investigation into the background of Ludwig. He submitted a request to the international police organization, Interpol, for help in checking the identity of Ludwig Walther and Konrad Schanz. Interpol's large international data-base could be helpful in identifying and locating people whether or not they were wanted or are known criminals.

The name, Konrad Schanz from Berlin generated a positive response in the Interpol data-base. Gleason and his crew would have to zero in on this name from credit card information to verify that this person visited Disney World during the December time period of the picture.

The name Ludwig Walther generated no responses in the Interpol database. However, the name Walther generated more responses than Gleason would be able to follow-up on. Gleason wondered how many of these Walthers were related to the legendary German gun manufacturer, but he couldn't wade through these hundreds of names searching for his needle in the haystack.

Gleason assumed that the Walthers and the Schanz were related or at least best of friends because of the use of only one credit card for their Disney vacation with three adjoining rooms. He reasoned that the easiest way to find Ludwig Walther's identity might be though the name Schanz.

A fire-wall with the code NUR 48 jumped up to block Gleason's access to the Interpol information on a Konrad Schanz living in Berlin. A phone call to his Treasury office in Washington brought an answer for the code NUR 48 that he wasn't prepared for, Nuremberg, 1948. Immediately Gleason's mind started to race wondering which side of the post-war Nazi war criminal trials Konrad Schanz was on. Tom was warned by his Washington office that he would need special clearance based on a legitimate reason for his need to access this restricted file.

He was also told that access to this classified file, once he had his clearance, was for his eyes only at the Interpol Records Center in Paris with no copies allowed outside the IRC. He was given the background information that the Nazis had assumed control of the Berlin based Interpol in 1938 and that it had been moved to Paris in 1946 after the war. During the Nazi controlled years from 1938 to 1945 Interpol was certainly part of the Nazi propaganda machine so any information from those years probably would have been altered to suit their needs. However, the fact that the Nazis were meticulous record keepers as evidenced by their incriminating death camp records, gave Gleason some hope that this classified file might yield some important information about the identity of Schanz and a possible familial relation to Walther.

Nevertheless, after getting off the phone with his Washington office, Gleason started to reverse his thinking that it might be easier to get at these two identities by going through all the Walthers listed rather than taking a trip to Paris and fighting the red tape of Interpol on the Konrad Schanz file.

XVIII

Ludwig's family photo was permanently engrained in Gleason's mind from so many viewings, so he was surprised when he noticed something previously undetected. This new item caused him to call the photographer, Katy, and ask her if the photographs are routinely touched-up, especially the eyes.

Her reply that the photos are not touched-up unless an extra fee is paid when they are ordered, which she was sure wasn't done because they paid cash to her at the time the picture was taken.

Gleason asked her if she had any idea how Ludwig's eyes could turn out to be different colors, one blue and the other dark brown. Her quick answer of, "What the camera sees, is what you get in the photo," reminded him of Joanne's same observation about Ludwig's different colored eyes when they were at Ludwig's house.

He pulled from his briefcase the picture he had taken of Ludwig's medicine cabinet shelf that showed a small bottle of eye-drops from a doctor in Miami and the bottle of Morphine from a doctor in Puerto Plata. The names on the two prescriptions were different. The morphine was in the name of Ludwig Walther, but the name on the eye-drops was Jacob Rosen. Gleason berated himself for not noticing the different names on the two prescriptions, but he attributed that slip-up to 'divine justice' because of his wife's displeasure at his snooping in Ludwig's medicine cabinet.

This eureka moment generated the need for more phone calls. The first was to Interpol requesting that they check their data-base for a Jacob Rosen. The second call was closer to where he was, the Disney CEO asking for a name check on Jacob Rosen during the time frame they were already investigating.

The third call to the pharmacy in Miami involved a little deception as Gleason knew that they would not release any personal information about Jacob Rosen over the phone. Gleason explained to the pharmacy clerk that since it was tax filing time he needed a copy of his pharmacy records and payments to prepare his income tax. The pharmacy clerk agreed to fax this information to Gleason. He didn't disclose that the fax number was to his Department of Treasury office.

Gleason found that this cat and mouse game helped to pass the time until the Disney CEO got back to him. When his phone rang Gleason was surprised that the call was from five time zones away in Paris. The Interpol operator read a short statement on Ludwig Walther that was identical to the message about Konrad Schanz. Access to information on Jacob Rosen was also denied under the same code, NUR 48. Gleason thought, 'Now I have more reasons to go to Paris, if the boss approves.'

By the time the Disney CEO finally called with the information that nothing was found on Jacob Rosen, Gleason had decided to return to Washington. However, the CEO reported that the Disney computer technicians were able to access thumbprints of the six people in the Schanz group on their second day entry into the Magic Kingdom. Thumbprints are used to verify park admittance on multi-day tickets so perhaps these prints could be used to trace the six people in the Schanz party. Gleason felt happy that he wasn't returning empty-handed to Washington.

XIX

It was unusual for Ludwig to receive personal faxes at his Brugal office so when he received two in the same day he was concerned. The first was from a number he recognized in Germany: "Suspicious inquiry on my American Express CC about our stay at Disney. Will cancel this CC and get a new one. KS." Ludwig's first reaction to this fax from Konrad Schanz in Germany, was that someone was trying to steal this credit card number or engage in an identity theft scheme until he read the second fax that came in later that morning:

"As requested we sent information on your eye-drop prescription #JR253819 to your accountant's fax number 202 342-1190." Ludwig immediately recognized the area code of 202 as being for Washington, D.C. because his son was still living there while attending Georgetown University. Ludwig was angry that his cover of Jacob Rosen was now on the desk of someone in Washington. He faxed the pharmacy a request that they send him a duplicate of their previous fax to the Washington number so that he could see the information sent to the Washington number. When that copy of the Washington fax arrived, he saw that the address and social security number of Jacob Rosen were on it.

Troubled, Ludwig told his secretary that he would be out of the office for the rest of the day. He drove to the Iberostar hotel where there was a secure international pay phone in the corner of the lobby. He called a number in Germany where he was connected to Konrad Schanz. Konrad relayed the news from his contact at the Interpol office in Paris that inquiries from the United States Treasury Department had been made about their sealed files. They discussed who would be trying to resurrect their past from the Interpol database and was it more than a mere coincidence that the credit card inquiry was happening at the same time? Ludwig and Konrad had gradually let down their defenses over the last few years and now someone was trying to penetrate the wall around their lives.

As Ludwig was concluding his hushed call to Germany, Carlos walked across the lobby and waited at the reception desk. They shook hands and walked outside under the porte-cochere to shield them from the mid-day shower that kept the Dominican landscape verdant all-year long. Carlos knew that Ludwig used the international payphone at the Iberostar to make important calls that he did not want traced back to him. Carlos sometimes had to bring coins from the front desk to Ludwig if his call was prolonged, but not today.

"I should wait to call Germany in the evening when the rates are lower," Ludwig commented to Carlos. "But then that would be the middle of the night over there when most everything is closed."

This was the first time that Ludwig ever mentioned where he was calling so Carlos surprised himself when he said, "You can always have your family call you when it is cheaper for them."

"Well, it's only money," Ludwig answered without admitting or denying that he had family in Europe, although he must have wondered how Carlos knew that he had family in there. "Have you heard anything from those Americans that we caught walking naked on my beach?"

"Not a thing from them, although I understand that the office had to send them one of their bathing suits that they left hanging on the bathroom door."

"Carlos, can you get the names and addresses of these people? They still owe me for the expensive Leica camera they broke."

Carlos nervously looked around to see if anyone was watching them near Ludwig's parked Mercedes. "I'll have to rely on my friend, the business manager, to get their names and addresses, which could cost us our jobs if we are caught. I have to pay him something before he does it."

Ludwig peeled off a $50.00 dollar bill from his money clip and gave it to Carlos. "I'll pick up those names from you in a couple days," Ludwig said as he drove away.

Carlos, smiling and laughing on the inside at having bested the richest person in Puerto Plata, put the $50.00 dollar bill under Gleason's business card in his money clip.

XX

Gleason had the usual trepidations while waiting to be shown into his boss's office because he knew he had an usual request to make. Fortunately, he hadn't waited long when the secretary opened the door for him to enter.

"You didn't get much of a tan in Florida, Gleason. Either too much time on the indoor rides at Disney World or too much time sitting on a bar stool."

"Unfortunately, neither of these account for my paleness. Sadly, I have to blame it on old-fashioned detective work, most of which was indoors."

"I'm impressed, Gleason. What can I do for you today?"

"I'm almost afraid to ask, especially since I'm just returning from my Disney vacation," Gleason said with a broad smile on his face. "I need to go to Paris to review two sealed records at the Interpol headquarters."

"Sure, let's just charter a jet and take the whole office to Paris! Seriously, what's this all about? I thought that we were investigating a petty counterfeiter in the Dominican Republic."

"We are, but he and the friend he was in Florida with have sealed Interpol records under the code name NUR 48. These records, with the required high level clearance, can be read only at the Interpol office."

"Sounds like you could be opening the proverbial can of worms. I remember another NUR 48 case a few years ago. It involved a war criminal convicted in the post-war Nuremberg Tribunal in 1948. Are you sure that we need to go there?"

"There are many questions that the Interpol files might answer." Gleason remained silent while his boss tilted back in his chair, considering the big picture of his requested Interpol visit to Paris.

"Okay, Gleason," the boss said as the chair straightened-up. "Here's what we can do. You should be here in D.C. in case the White House calls about your reassignment, so I am going to assign someone from our Paris office to go to Interpol."

"I would be gone only a couple days once we get the necessary clearance," Gleason pleaded.

"This counterfeiting connection still sounds like a bit of a wild goose chase, so I don't want you wasting your time going to Paris. I'll put you in touch with Jacqueline LeBeau, one of our senior agents in Paris. She works with Interpol all the time. Tell her what you are looking for so she can make her formal request for clearance."

"Yes, sir, I look forward to working with her." Gleason quickly left the room before his boss changed his mind and totally scuttled the mission.

Gleason was in Miami, rather than in his first choice—Paris, armed with the necessary search warrants, to talk to the eye doctor and the pharmacy that had treated Ludwig under the name of Jacob Rosen.

The pharmacy clerk and the pharmacist could not or would not add anything beyond what their previously faxed eye-drop prescription showed except the clerk did recall that the man was polite and well-dressed with a coat and tie, which was unusual because most of their customers wore Bermuda shorts and polo shirts.

Even after being shown the court order, the eye doctor was still hesitant to release Ludwig's record until Gleason unclipped a pair of handcuffs from his belt and asked the doctor to put his hands out. The doctor quickly told his office girl to retrieve the Jacob Rosen chart.

She returned shortly with a rather thin chart that she handed to Gleason. "Is this all of his chart? Do you have any of it, an older part, stored off-site?"

"We don't have any off-site storage," she meekly replied. "Most of our patients are elderly and we don't have to keep their records very long. I do have his financial ledger filed separately. Do you want to see it?"

"If you please. Also any credit card receipts. Doctor, I see on your chart that you have noted the two different colors of Mr. Rosen's eyes. Does this color difference happen in many people?"

"Let me see the chart... Mr. Rosen is being treated for glaucoma in one eye, which is rare as usually both eyes have glaucoma. The glaucoma eye-drop medicine has changed the color of that treated eye to bark brown, nearly black as I noted. His natural eye color is blue like the untreated eye."

The office girl returned with Rosen's financial ledger card and two curled-up credit card receipts. "Mr. Rosen is due for his semi-annual check-up so what do we do if he calls for an appointment? It'll be hard to treat him without his records," the doctor commented with a definite edge to his voice.

"You're right. Make a copy of everything, but I need to take the originals with me. By the way, you are not to have any contact with him, unless he calls you, in which case you are to notify me immediately. Is that clear?"

The office girl and the doctor both nodded their heads, although Gleason noticed that the doctor was much less enthusiastic which was a red flag for Gleason. When he got to his car he ordered a phone tap on the doctor's office and home phone numbers.

Gleason carefully studied the eye doctor's records on his return flight to Washington. There were a number of erasures and cross-outs that his lab should be able to decipher to determine what was originally written along with the nearly illegible doctor's handwriting. The smudged erasure under the name Rosen had Gleason very curious as to what name was first written there.

Gleason was in his office early the next morning when the summons from on high came for him to report immediately. The boss was working at the credenza behind his desk with his back to the door when Gleason entered. He spun around and shouted, "What have you gotten us into?"

Gleason was reluctant to sit down until he was asked to. His only reply was a shrug of his shoulders.

"Ms. LeBeau had just received her clearance to view the Interpol files. She was waiting for a bus to take her to the Interpol office when a car jumped the curb and ran over her. She died instantly and the car sped away."

"A freak accident?" Gleason wondered.

"The police are doubtful that it was an accident because witnesses, some standing at the bus stop, saw the car accelerate to jump the curb and then deliberately steer into her. The stolen car was found abandoned a few blocks away."

"I'm sorry Boss....that should've been me."

The next day Gleason was in touch with his Interpol contact about a possible mole in their Paris office who could arrange the murder of a United States Department of Treasury Agent in broad daylight. Gleason did not want to take the focus off of Interpol in the death of Agent Lebeau. Gleason figured that Interpol owed the United States for this loss of life and that the U.S. would not risk another life to inspect the files that could be just as easily sent to them. As his contact was vacillating about getting permission to fax the requested files to Washington, Gleason let it be known that these file transfers were non-negotiable and must happen immediately to prevent future murders, like his wife's he thought to himself. Since this request had possible personal ramifications, Gleason would not take no for an answer. The only concession Gleason made was that the confidential files would be destroyed when the case was closed.

XXI

The reality of the death, probably murder, of Agent LeBeau in Paris hit Gleason so hard that Cindy noticed he was not himself at the dinner table. They had promised each other a few months before, as their wedding date approached, they would not bring their jobs home to burden each other with their own problems. They had lived-up to that promise for the first few weeks of their marriage. However, tonight Cindy could not bear to see Tom so frustrated and short-tempered. She sat down next to him on the sofa with two glasses of his favorite after dinner wine.

"Timeout," she said. "Tell me what has you so upset that you could hardly eat."

Tom didn't know whether to scream or stay silent so he took a long sip of the wine and gave Cindy a hug. Finally, he mentioned their agreement of work-place silence, which she dismissed with a flick of her hand.

He was teary-eyed as he told the story of the young agent in Paris, Jacqueline LeBeau, who died because of him and probably in his place.

Tom tried to reassure her that his current job of tracking down counterfeiters was less dangerous than his future posting in the Presidential Protection Detail, so she should not worry about him.

"This has to involve more than the counterfeiting that you discovered on our honeymoon," Cindy astutely surmised. "Why did they single out her?"

He knew that he had to be careful in talking about official business with even his wife, so he said, "She was headed over to the Interpol office to check out two names we sent her."

"There must be a spy in the Interpol office who was aware of what she was going to do and didn't want her to do it," Cindy said.

Tom nodded his head and hugged Cindy even stronger as he realized that Cindy was aware of his dangerous job and his current state of mind. "Maybe I shouldn't mention it, Tom, but we had a strange call for me at college today. By the time I picked up the phone, the caller was gone. The secretary said that it was an international call and sounded important to her. The caller asked the secretary if I worked at the college and said he would hold for me. I seldom get any calls at college and never international ones. When I answered, no one was on the line. "

Tom sat up on the sofa but still held Cindy tightly as he said, "I'm going to have the Department trace that call. It certainly is a strange coincidence with the Paris accident." Tom was doing his best to control his anger knowing that his wife may be targeted by the unknown forces he was pursuing.

Before retiring Gleason called the Treasury Department's 24-hour emergency hot line with the request to trace Cindy's international phone call. The clerk told him they could have an answer when he arrived at work in the morning. This information made for a restless night's sleep due to his eager anticipation of getting to work to discover the origin of this strange phone call.

XXII

The day-to-day job for most Treasury Department agents is usually mundane and often downright boring in spite of how glamorous it appears to the public. The agents in the Presidential Protective Division have stressful days when the president is out of the protective cocoon of the White House. Otherwise, they are desk jockeys riding herd on piles of paperwork concerning past and future presidential trips or monitoring the guests coming to the White House.

However, Gleason was breaking this mold with all the balls he was currently juggling. The first ball to land on his desk was the answer to his request to trace the mysterious call his wife received at her college. The answer was a terse government memo stating the call's time of day and date that were consistent with Cindy's call: Pay Phone - Lobby - Iberostar Resort - Puerto Plata - Dominican Republic.

He remembered giving Carlos his business card when they were checking out. It had his and his wife's contact information on it, so Carlos could have called her school number trying to reach him. 'One way to find out,' he thought, so he called the front desk at the Iberostar hoping that Carlos was at his concierge desk.

Gleason was put on hold while Carlos was being located.

Gleason got right to the point when Carlos came to the phone. "Carlos, did you recently call my wife at her college using the pay phone in the hotel lobby?"

"No, sir, Mr. Gleason. Many people use this phone in our lobby to make international calls."

Gleason gave Carlos the date and time of the phone call and asked if he was working that day.

Carlos asked for a minute while he looked at a calendar to jog his memory on his work schedule. "Yes, I was working that day and I remember someone making a phone call about that time."

" How can you be sure?

"Even though the call was very short, the caller still needed me to bring him some coins from the front desk cash drawer."

"Do you know who made that call?"

"It was Ludwig. He often uses this payphone for international calls."

"Why does he do that? He certainly has his own phones that he could use."

"He tells me that it's cheaper than his house phone and he has the privacy in case his home phone is bugged. Our phone lines in the Dominican Republic are not always private," Carlos said.

"That's great! Somebody could be listening to this call."

"Probably not as the hotel just installed an enhanced phone security system."

"I hope you're right, otherwise, we all could be in trouble. Why'd the hotel do this?" Gleason asked.

"The hotel manager told the staff the reason was all the important people who stay here demand privacy. He told me privately that his good friend Ludwig especially wanted it so his calls could not be listened to."

""Has Ludwig travelled out of the country recently?'

"I don't think so. He mentioned that he was going to Miami in a few days for a doctor's appointment."

Gleason tried to appear solicitous about Ludwig's well-being, even though he knew the visit probably was to his eye doctor friend, "Has he been sick?"

"Not that I know of. It's probably a chance for his wife to go shopping."

"Can't blame her for that. Carlos, let's stay in touch. Goodbye."

. . . .

Gleason could see another line blinking on his phone, so he answered it only to be put on hold while the secretary transferred the call to her boss, the CEO of Disney World. "Gleason, you have put us through a lot of work answering your questions, but it's worth it, as it shows us that we have to upgrade our record keeping."

"So what did you find out?"

Gleason learned that the Disney World reservation for six people had an address in the Dominican Republic of the Brugal rum distillery in Puerto Plata, but was being held by a credit card with a different name and an address in Germany.

The thing that got Gleason's attention was the CEO's explanation of the newly installed thumb-print verifier that a holder of a multi-day ticket had to use to prove he was the valid holder of such a multi-day ticket. The CEO said the system had captured the thumbprints of all six members in this party and he promised to send these prints and the rest of his information by overnight mail to Washington. Gleason was hopeful when the thumbprints were run through the government's national data-base the true identities of these six people could be established.

Gleason was still awaiting the files from Interpol, which he hoped could be correlated with his other domestic findings.

With all the business phone calls he was receiving, Gleason was pleased to see the unusual incoming call from his wife—until he talked to her. She was getting ready to head home for the day and she thought back to her morning commute on the D.C. Metro subway. "I think someone was following me on my way to work," she said trying to control the anxiety in her voice.

"Why didn't you call me earlier?"

"I forgot about it when I got busy at work. The strangest part was that he had a small camera and was taking pictures inside the moving Metro train. Some of the pictures seemed to be aimed in my direction."

"What did he look like and did he follow you all the way to your office?"

"We got off at the same Metro stop. He was dressed like any college student in a dark navy pea jacket with a white scarf covering half his face and wearing a Georgetown hat. He could have been just checking out our Catholic University campus. He didn't follow me into my building."

"Stay at your office until I send one of our interns over to shadow you on the Metro ride home. Watch for the pea coat guy and don't stand close to the track of your arriving train. I'll try to get home a little early for dinner."

Gleason used the term intern to try to lessen Cindy's fear that would have been heightened if he had said armed agents would follow her home. He didn't want to personally escort Cindy home, which would alert any possible stalker that they were on to him.

He went down the hall to the local D.C. Treasury office and asked two agents, fully armed, to shadow his wife home on the Metro looking for the possible stalker and take a picture of him. He also instructed the agents to remain with Cindy until he got home after work.

A thick packet in a secure diplomatic pouch arrived in Gleason's office as he was preparing to head home to meet his wife and the two agents. He signed for the documents and returned the pouch to the courier. 'Oh, shit,' he said to himself as he realized that his promise to his wife to get home early would be broken if he started to delve into the just-arrived Interpol reports.

His other option was to bring the classified Interpol packet home, which violated their newlywed's promise of not bringing work home. Rather than getting home late, he picked the work-at-home option and he would beg for Cindy's forbearance later. He stuffed the report in his locked briefcase which had a chain connected to a wrist bracelet to prevent a snatch and run theft on his Metro ride home.

Gleason held onto the handle of his briefcase a little tighter than normally for his Metro ride home even though someone would have to amputate his arm to make off with the briefcase. If he could find a seat, he often read reports or did other paperwork on the Metro, but today would not be one of those days because of the classified material in his briefcase.

When he exited the Metro he was on a heightened sense of awareness himself as he looked for anyone or anything unusual on the familiar two block walk home through his changing neighborhood. Most of the empty nesters had sold their homes to multinational families with younger children, so he always teased Cindy that their children would be raised in a United Nations neighborhood with playmates of all nationalities. He gave a discrete hand wave to one of the agents fumbling with a Washington Post paper machine before turning the corner of his street. He was relieved to notice that the front porch light was on, which was their signal to each other that one of them was home and all was okay. When Tom stepped into the vestibule, Cindy and the other shadowing agent were having an animated discussion about a young man wearing a navy pea jacket with no scarf and a Miami Dolphins hat who hurried to board the same crowded Metro car as Cindy. She could not be sure this was the same person she saw this morning since his morning face was mostly hidden by his coat collar and the white scarf. The agent managed to get two photographs of this possible stalker, but neither was a full frontal picture.

The agent commented that when he saw this young man preparing to get off at the same Metro stop as Cindy he barged between the two them and the other agent was immediately behind the three of them. They had a clandestine parade up the escalator until they got to street level where the young man lagged behind until he disappeared into a coffee shop.

• • • •

When the agent left, Cindy turned out the porch light and embraced Tom with a rib cracking hug and a prolonged kiss that left him gasping for air before he had a chance to unhook himself from the tethered briefcase. This was Cindy's alternative to collapsing into a sobbing rag doll that Tom would have to maneuver to the living room sofa.

"Tom, please tell me what's going on."

He pointed to the briefcase that he was still holding. "Remember I told you about our agent in Paris who was run over at the bus stop? She was going to the Interpol office to investigate the reports inside the briefcase. If I study them tonight, I might be able to answer your question."

"Feel free to get started while I whip-up dinner."

He headed into his office off the vestibule and detached himself from the briefcase that was becoming heavier by the minute. He wondered, 'What was so damn important inside this briefcase that caused a young agent to be killed?' The Paris police were still calling it an accidental vehicular death, but Tom in his heart knew it was a cold-blooded murder. All he had to do was find a motive in the reports contained in the briefcase.

When he quickly leafed through the pages two unplanned issues confronted him. The first was that the reports were written in at least five languages he could recognize: French, German, Italian, Polish and English. Obviously, English would be no problem, and he had a reading knowledge of French and Italian from his seminary days where he studied them as derivative Romance languages from the mother-tongue Latin.

A dilemma faced him: Cindy had a knowledge of Polish from her family upbringing and she studied German to be able to read German philosophers for her PhD. studies. He decided since she was already involved, he would bring her on as a language consultant to help expedite this investigation.

The second more disturbing issue was an official Interpol memo that was the last page of this portfolio stating this was only the material on one of the requested names, Konrad Schanz. The material on the second requested name, Ludwig Walther, would be delayed because of a confused identity issue and this file was sealed at the request of Germany, Switzerland and the Vatican. Tom was immediately suspicious this delay was to give some rogue agent from one of these countries time to purge the file of embarrassing material.

Most of the multi-language reports and memos under the formal letterhead: 'Nuremberg Proceedings' had cover letters written in English that Tom hoped were summaries and conclusions that would negate the need for translating all these legal court documents.

Cindy's delivery of a glass of wine was the perfect opportunity for Tom to explain what he had learned in his quick once-through of the extensive Interpol file. She was not overly eager to infringe on this possibly secret, for sure confidential, material.

He explained it was his option because of the foreign languages involved to get the help he needed to investigate the case. They clinked their wine glasses when he mentioned he would run it by his boss the first chance he had.

His offer to help cleanup the kitchen was waved-off by a quick peck on his wine-flushed cheek and a flick of her head toward his study. Before dinner he had ascertained the documents were in chronological order, so he numbered the pages in the upper right hand corner with a red pen. Early in his career he had wasted many hours chronologically reconstructing the voluminous paperwork of a complicated investigation, and he wasn't going to make that same mistake again.

As he had surmised, the cover letter on each stapled mini-packet seemed to contain a summary of that packet's content. When Cindy appeared at the office door, the kitchen obviously cleaned-up, Tom stacked the now numbered packets and moved them to the sofa between them.

"Well, what have you discovered so far without the help of my translating expertise?"

"I requested information from Interpol on Ludwig Walther and another person named Konrad Schanz, who was with him when the Disney World picture was taken."

Tom described how when World War II ended, many German officials tried to assume new identities by changing their names and not returning to their former homes. Some of the most notorious Nazis, like Adolf Eichmann and Dr. Josef Mengele managed to escape to South America in spite of the Allies' efforts to capture them. Many of the lower level SS officers tried to hide from the victorious Allies' search for them by changing their names, as seems to be the case with Konrad Schanz. Schanz was from a middle class family in Berlin named Katz, with a brother and two sisters. The father was the third generation running the family brewery that supplied beer to the higher-ups in the Hitler regime, so they must have been politically connected to the Third Reich. The father was a Major in the German army serving on the Western front.

"Tom, can you please get to the heart of the matter. I have term papers to grade tonight," Cindy interrupted Tom's meandering narrative.

Tom smiled. He knew that he had to refocus to hold Cindy's attention. "This Nuremberg file is on Konrad Schanz, whose real name was Reinhard Katz before he changed it after the War. He appears to be the mysterious companion of Ludwig at Disney World. The file lists Katz's SS service as a census taker, then at a prison camp where old Jewish engravers and printers were producing counterfeit English, German, and even American money. However, the report seems to focus on Katz's activities in Warsaw. The name Irena Sendler is mentioned a few times."

"My parents used to talk about what a hero Sendler was for saving over 2,000 Jewish children from the Nazis."

"In 1942, Schanz was assigned to Warsaw as a low level SS officer with the specific job of monitoring Sendler's activities in the Warsaw Social Welfare Department," Tom said.

"Our parish, when I was growing up, hired an old Polish priest from Warsaw who told us about Sendler, who was not Jewish, placing Jewish children from the Ghetto with non-Jewish families.

They changed the children's Jewish names to hide them from the Nazis. She kept lists of these rescued children in glass jars buried under an apple tree in a neighbor's back yard with the hope that these children and parents could be reunited after the war."

"That was quite brave of her. I wonder how many of the parents survived the death camps to be reunited with their children Sendler rescued?" Tom questioned with neither of them wanting to dwell on the depressing answer.

Tom handed Cindy a few reports written in Polish while he worked on the English ones. After an extended period of silent-study, Cindy put together a timetable of Sendler's activities as related to SS member Reinhard Katz, now known as Konrad Schanz.

The Germans, in early 1942, were aware that many Jewish children were disappearing from the Warsaw Ghetto. Sendler was betrayed to the Nazis by a co-worker in the Warsaw Social Welfare office. Fortunately, the betraying co-worker didn't know the full extent of Sendler's clandestine rescue efforts, especially where the buried records were located, but she revealed enough to get Sendler arrested by the SS in 1943.

Sendler was imprisoned, tortured, and given a death sentence by a sham Polish court without revealing her secrets about the rescued Jewish children. Someone in the SS was bribed by the Polish resistance to allow Sendler to escape from prison before the death sentence could be carried out. Katz testified in his own defense at his Nuremberg War Tribunal trial that he was the one who was bribed to allow Sendler to escape by giving her a key to her jail cell. After Sendler's escape from prison, Katz was transferred back to Berlin, so he was not forced to pursue her for the duration of the war.

Sendler survived the war in hiding and testified at the Nuremberg trials in 1948 against many of the SS agents who had brutalized her and the Jews in Warsaw. She had no knowledge of Katz personally torturing or killing Jews and she speculated that he must have been the person in authority who allowed her to escape.

After the war, Katz with his new name of Konrad Schanz,

attempted to flee from Germany to Switzerland where the family bankers were going to help him get established. Claiming to be of French descent with poorly forged papers, he was arrested by the allies' border guards as soon as he removed his shirt for a strip-search. The tattoo on the inner side of his upper left arm was a dead giveaway of his SS membership. Tom showed Cindy a picture of the incriminating SS tattoo that was enclosed as a separate exhibit.

"So what's the big deal about this tattoo? It looks like a few random letters, not his name or a serial number like the concentration camp prisoners."

"That's right, the numbered concentration camp tattoos were on the top side of their left forearm. Himmler ordered all SS agents to have their blood type tattooed in this upper arm location so they could be given blood quickly in an emergency. The notorious Auschwitz Angel of Death, Josef Mengele, escaped the Allies' feverous attempts to find him because, he didn't have this incriminating tattoo, in violation of Himmler's order."

Tom was able to periodically continue his narrative to Cindy as most of the Nuremberg report was in English. As the evening of intense reading of the Nuremberg reports wore on it became apparent to Cindy that she was out of her element. She still needed to tackle her own stack of term papers so she asked, "Do you see anything in here that merits your agent in Paris getting killed?"

Her question caught Tom by surprise, yet it was the reality-check he needed as it expressed her deep concern. "Remember, this is only half of the information that we requested. We still need the report on Ludwig. Perhaps Konrad Schanz wants to keep this Nuremberg report of his former SS life as Reinhard Katz hidden, even though he was acquitted at his Nuremberg trial. The Tribunal must have believed Sendler when she said that Katz was the one who allowed her to escape using his jail cell key that she saved and presented as evidence at Katz's Tribunal trial. Katz in his own defense had the family's Geneva bankers send the Tribunal the duplicate jail cell key that he had sent them for safe keeping at the time of Sendler's escape. When the two keys of Sendler and Katz were determined to be a match, Katz was acquitted of all charges at Nuremberg.

Schanz, with the incriminating under-arm tattoo, could not deny his SS affiliation, but not all SS members were automatically found guilty at Nuremberg. Nevertheless, Tom felt certain that Schanz would still find his SS background embarrassing even if he had been a law-abiding citizen since the war. The report's latest update listed Konrad Schanz as living in Berlin and working at the family brewing business, where he was using his former name, Reinhard Katz without officially changing his legal name, Konrad Schanz.

XXIII

Gleason was delayed getting to his office the next day not so much because of his late evening study of the Interpol file on Konrad Schanz but because he rode the Metro with Cindy to her job in case the stalker was again on her trail. Fortunately, Cindy did not recognize anyone on the commute that she felt was this person. Nevertheless, Gleason left her with the instruction to avoid the Metro and take a cab home tonight after work.

Gleason also diverted to one of his favorite places in all of D.C., the Antiquities Forever store on H Street in the shadow of his Treasury Department office. Many have theorized this cluttered basement store, specializing in old books, is named after its octogenarian owner, Isaac Perlman, who greeted Gleason at the bottom of the creaky stairway, "What case can I help you solve today?"

Everyone in D.C. knew Perlman was a walking authority on Nazi Germany as most of his family was lost in the holocaust, and he survived a death camp because of a trade that was passed on for generations in his family. The fact that he was a master engraver and printer in the family lithography business most likely saved him from the death camps of Nazi Germany.

The majority of printers in Germany were Jewish and the elite of them elevated themselves to become master engravers. The need to keep reproducing the ancient Jewish manuscripts certainly was one incentive to perpetuate this important skill which bordered on being a true art form. When Perlman's failing eye-sight started to obviate his familial engraving skills and the dreadful realization that none of his family were returning from the death camps finally permeated his being, Perlman moved to the Washington, D.C. area to start a new life and to be near the National Holocaust Museum being established near the Washington Mall.

Gleason always felt the need when dealing with Perlman to obtusely approach the real reason for his current visit so as not to send him back into the trauma of his war years. Today, he asked what he thought was an innocuous question, "Did Hitler have a leather bound limited edition of Mein Kampf printed?" Gleason knew the answer to his question as he remembered seeing a copy of it on Ludwig's bookshelf when they were getting the tour of Ludwig's seaside mansion.

Perlman's chin crashed into his chest like he'd been smacked on the back of his head. A feeble hand fumbled to remove a crumpled handkerchief from a pant pocket to dry the tears from the corner of his eyes.

What Gleason was trying to avoid, happened. He would have done anything to take his question back. He lowered his head to follow Perlman as he slowly knelt behind the counter and shuffled some musty boxes around. Suddenly dust flew as two books with cracking brown leather covers were plopped on the counter by a trembling hand. Perlman used the counter to pull himself to an upright position. "How many do you want? I have been meaning to burn these copies of the Mein Kampf like Hitler did to my family."

Gleason went around the counter and gave Perlman a steadying hug. "I'm sorry," was the only consolation he could offer.

"Thank you for reminding me to get the garbage out of the store."

Gleason brushed the dust and cobwebs off two stools behind the counter before they sat down. Perlman pointed out the gold embossed numerals 88 and 100 on the cracking spines of the books. Book 100 was signed by Hitler but book 88 was both signed and inscribed by Hitler, 'To Eva. Love, 88.' "My father printed one hundred copies of these evil books for Hitler. The Third Reich, and for sure not Hitler never paid my father for these one hundred books so he saved the final copy 100 thinking that it would be valuable after the war and he could sell it to get paid. He never lived to sell it as he and my family were hauled away to the Auschwitz resettlement camp as the Nazis called them. Now, I just want to destroy them so no one else can read Hitler's lies."

"Why did Hitler give book number 88 to his girl friend, Eva?"

"Because he was a sick egomaniac and Eva went along with it, even marrying him. H is the eighth letter of the alphabet so 88 is an abbreviation for Heil Hitler."

"How did you come into possessing Eva's copy 88? It should have burned with them in his bunker."

"Eva gave it to a friend for safekeeping in the last days of the war. This friend returned it to me after the war since she knew our family had printed it, but mostly because she didn't want it as evidence that she was a Nazi sympathizer."

"Why weren't you taken away with your family to the concentration camps?"

"The protection of Yahweh and my skill as a master engraver kept me out of the death camps. I spent the war years in one of the prison work camps engraving plates to counterfeit the British pound notes and later we switched to other currencies, even the U.S. dollar. Hitler thought he could destabilize England and the United States by counterfeiting their money."

"What happened to the other books?"

"I hope they're destroyed—all of them! However, occasionally a copy comes up for sale at an auction." Perlman scribbled the letters 99 on a scratch pad. Before Gleason could respond Perlman said, "The copy I would like to find is ninety-nine or I should say the original owner of copy ninety-nine."

"What's so special about copy ninety-nine?"

Isaac's chin again sank to his chest. Gleason realized he had asked another wrong question—or maybe it was the right question for his needs.

"Bastards! I'd kill the original owner who still has book ninety-nine after all these years," Perlman said as his chin again fell to his chest.

Gleason nodded his head, keeping pace with his swaying body on the uncomfortable stool, waiting for Isaac to break the oppressive silence. Gleason saw Isaac dab tears from the corners of his eyes as his head slowly rose to speak.

"They barged into my father's shop a few days before the SS raided it and took my family away because we were Jewish."

"Who's they?" Gleason meekly asked.

"Jewish acquaintances of the family, who rarely attended the Temple. The father and his two sons in Nazi SS uniforms came to the printing shop to get one of the special Mein Kampf copies 'while we were still around,' they said, so my father gave them copy ninety-nine to get them out of the shop. Bastards!"

"If they were Jewish, how could the sons be in the elite SS?"

"They were friends with all the Nazi leaders who belonged to the Berlin Golf Club, where Jews were not allowed as members unless you were quarter-Jewish or less, which they were. The Nazi leaders must have assumed that they were not Jewish. The boys played golf all summer while my kids worked in our printing shop."

"Where did the family get the money to do this?" Gleason asked.

"The family owned a brewery that supplied Hitler and his friends with free beer. They were only quarter-Jewish and the laws were different for them than for us real Jews as our family found out a few days later when the SS raided us and hauled my family away. My father tried to tell the SS he was a friend of Hitler and even showed them this Hitler-signed book one hundred of Mein Kampf published by SS Publishing in Berlin. The SS Captain threw it on the floor and stomped on it."

Gleason picked up the book numbered one hundred and could almost see the heel marks ground into the once supple leather cover. "What's this family's name?"

"Do I have to say it? I haven't said it since the war. It makes me sick because they, especially the sons in the SS, sold out our people."

"So what did the sons do during the War? Certainly not work in the death camps killing their own people."

"You'd be surprised at what our people were forced to do in the death camps. Those that were healthy enough had to work in the crematoriums that killed our people. Katz was their German name that helped them pass as non-Jews even though the name Katz can also be Jewish."

"Did the father and his sons survive the War?"

"Praise Yahweh, the father died at the Battle of the Bulge. I heard the boys changed their names after the war like many former SS members. The younger brother, Reinhard, was found and tried at Nuremberg. Surprisingly he was one of the few SS members acquitted at Nuremberg."

"Was the older brother ever tried at Nuremberg?

"The last that I heard about the older brother was that he was serving with the SS in Rome after doing some terrible things in a children's mental hospital. He mysteriously disappeared before the war ended and was classified a deserter by the failing Nazi government. The German government says they are still looking for him along with hundreds of other war criminals. However, I don't think our current government in Germany is trying very hard to catch these murderers."

Hoping to avoid sending Isaac into another depressing flashback, Gleason opened-up Book 100 to the title page and noticed the publisher's name, SS PUBLISHING BERLIN. He was expecting an explanation from Isaac on why the family had seemingly sold-out to the Nazis by naming the family publishing company SS Publishing. Isaac, seeing the questioning look on Tom's face, smiled and related the short family history that his grandfather was named Samuel as was his father, so they decided to name the business SS Publishing long before the hated Nazi SS arrived on the scene.

Gleason was surprised when Perlman agreed to let the two books out of his store for an overnight visit to Gleason's office with a flick of his hand and the comment, "I'm probably better off with them out of my sight."

"I'll bring them back tomorrow in case anyone wants to buy them," Gleason said as he headed for the stairway. On the street he scanned the store's entry-way for a location of a hidden camera to document everyone entering and leaving the store. He didn't want to alarm Isaac with the request to put the camera inside the store.

XXIV

Gleason's short walk from Isaac's basement dungeon to his office in the Department of Treasury office building next to the White House traversed Lafayette Park. The two-signed copies of Mein Kampf in his briefcase were the perfect example of why the country needs Lafayette Park. The placard carrying protestors, in the former front yard of the White House, were always a centering-influence for Gleason when he found himself wandering too far astray from his assigned task of protecting the country. He politely refused all the protest flyers thrust at him as his briefcase contained enough motivation for him to right the world even though he silently wished he was idealistic and young again, when all problems could be solved by a protest march.

Riding the elevator up to his office, he knew he had to follow-up on Isaac's information with Interpol. He was sure the name Katz would generate positive hits in Interpol's database since the name Katz was a common name in Europe. However, his main concern was what subsequent collateral damage this Katz search request might cause, like his first search request for Schanz which seemed to trigger the auto death of the Interpol investigator.

His secretary stopped him before he could slip past her into his office. "Mr. Gleason, you have a caller on line one from the

Dominican Republic who insisted on holding for you."

He nodded his appreciation and closed his office door to talk to one of the two people who might be calling from the Dominican Republic, Carlos or Ludwig. He was relieved when he picked up the phone and recognized Carlos's accent since he was not prepared to talk to Ludwig.

Carlos explained that Ludwig told him he was going to Miami in a few days for a doctor's appointment and his wife wanted to visit their children. Gleason didn't know whether to feel happy or apprehensive that Ludwig was scheduled to come to Florida.

Gleason tried to be nonchalant when he asked Carlos where Ludwig's children lived? Carlos told Gleason that the son still lived in Washington, D.C. after graduating from Georgetown's School of Foreign Service and the daughter, married to an options trader, lived in the Chicago area.

Gleason assumed Ludwig would be entering the United States through the busy International Terminal in Miami. Gleason's call to the eye doctor in Miami confirmed that, indeed, Ludwig had an appointment a few days hence, so Gleason felt comfortable in alerting the Miami Customs and Immigration of Ludwig's impending arrival. He warned Dr. Eggert's secretary against any contact with Ludwig before his scheduled appointment. The secretly wiretapped office phone would help Gleason monitor this request, but Gleason was unaware of the emergency contact plans previously established by Ludwig between the eye doctor and himself.

Ludwig's clandestine communications with Dr. Eggert convinced Ludwig Gleason was snooping around his identity. Thus his trip to Miami would be monitored closely by Gleason and whatever government agency he worked for. Ludwig kept his and Naomi's flight reservation to Miami, but he knew that he had to make other arrangements to get to the United States.

Rafael Hernandez Airport at Aquadilla on the western tip of Puerto Rico was Ludwig's airport of choice when he needed to go about his private business anywhere in the Americas or Europe. Two days before his scheduled flight reservation to Miami, he and his wife flew by a charter flight from a small airfield near Sosua to Aquadilla where he would catch a private jet charter flight to anywhere in the world under an assumed name on the flight's manifesto. Over the years, travelling as a wealthy businessman, this modus operandi had allowed him to secretly visit Argentina, Europe, and the United States many times without detection.

The manager of the small fixed base terminal at Rafael Hernandez Airport referred to Ludwig as 'Senor Grand Propina.' Ludwig always instructed the manager to spread the large tip around his handful of workers to insure he always received the best discrete service.

A flight plan was filed to Chicago. This would allow Naomi to visit their daughter in addition to the benefit of landing away from an Atlantic coast airport where Gleason might be looking for him flying in from the Dominican Republic. Ludwig anonymously could take a train or bus from Chicago to New York or Washington, D.C. as he had done in the past. He was becoming increasingly more paranoid about flying the commercial airlines in the United States because of their ability to identify and track his travel regardless of what name he used.

The Miami Customs and Immigration officials were on high alert at the time of Ludwig's scheduled flight arrival. Gleason was secreted in a small room behind a two-way mirror which allowed him to screen all the arriving passengers as they walked by. When Ludwig did not pass-by with the deplaning passengers from the Dominican Republic, Gleason went into a mini-panic and called the airline to verify if Ludwig and his wife were aboard this flight. He momentarily relaxed when he was told that Ludwig and his wife never boarded the flight in the Dominican Republic, so he notified the Customs and Immigration people that they would not be arriving as originally planned.

The local Secret Service agent who was in charge of this Miami operation received a phone call from the Miami police while meeting with Gleason. The caller stated that the eye doctor's office building had burned to the ground the previous night and as yet an unidentified body had been found in the ruins.

Gleason realized he had to call Carlos to check if he knew anything about Ludwig's whereabouts. Fortunately, Carlos was at the
Iberostar's concierge desk when Gleason called. He told Gleason
that Ludwig hadn't been to the last two cockfights. These absences
only happened when Ludwig was gone from the island. Beyond
that Carlos said he would talk to his friends at the Brugal Rum
factory to see what they knew about Ludwig's absence.

XXV

Gleason's evening phone call home to Cindy from Miami startled him when she asked the simple question, "Is it possible that Ludwig is in Washington?"

He hoped she didn't hear him mumble under his breath, 'Oh, Shit,' as he struggled to maintain his composure, not wanting to alarm her. Per departmental policy he had not told her the reason for his quick trip to Miami, but now he felt compelled to inform her he was in Miami to greet Ludwig and his wife when they deplaned from their Dominican Republic flight; since that scenario never materialized, he told her Ludwig could be anywhere.

Cindy became pensively quiet as Tom tried to reassure her that it probably was not Ludwig she saw in the window of the coffee shop as she descended on the escalator to board the Metro. He had almost talked himself into believing his own soothing words, but he could feel Cindy's negative vibrations coming over the phone lines wondering, 'What have I gotten myself into by marrying Tom?'

Nevertheless, Tom promised to be on the first flight home in the morning. She should stay home until he got there. She was somewhat placated when he promised to post a guard outside their house for the night.

Gleason did not bother to check into a hotel because he knew even if he didn't have work to do—mainly trying to track-down Ludwig—he would be too wired to sleep. He elected to work the phones at the Department of Treasury's Miami office until his 6 AM flight back to D.C.

Carlos sounded more relaxed when Gleason reached him at his home away from the possible listening ears at the hotel. Carlos had learned from his friends at the Brugal Distillery that Ludwig hadn't been to work for nearly a week. His missing the last two cockfights and the fact he hadn't played golf in over a week, left a window of time for Ludwig's departure which Gleason was very uncomfortable with.

"I suppose he could have jumped on a cruise ship or a private yacht to get off the island," Gleason light-heartedly suggested to Carlos.

"Never, not Ludwig. Too slow for him to get where he's going." Carlos remembered that Ludwig once told him about taking his family to the surfing beaches at Aquadilla in nearby Puerto Rico by a private plane and that they stayed at some other rum-maker's villa on the beach.

Gleason thought how convenient to leave the Dominican Republic from a small airfield on a private plane and land at a small airfield in Puerto Rico. No need to clear customs or even have a passport. Since Puerto Rico has been referred to as the 51st state, passage from there to the mainland US is simpler than entry from other Caribbean Islands. Discussing small airfields near Puerto Plata, Carlos mentioned the busiest one was probably the one near the small Jewish settlement of Sosua, where a few wealthy locals kept their private airplanes. Sosua natives who made it big in the United States often would fly their private planes back to Sosua to visit friends and relatives where the airport manager doubled as a Customs and Immigration officer for the D.R. and the United States. This obvious conflict of representing both countries certainly played into the hands of anyone offering a generous handout to cover-up illegal activities like drug smuggling and immigration issues.

Carlos's offer to snoop around the small airport to check on the possible departure of Ludwig was a good omen to Gleason that Carlos was not interested in protecting Ludwig, especially since the $50.00 bill Ludwig had given him as a tip turned out to be of no value because it was counterfeit.

During his long all-night phone vigil, Gleason checked-in hourly with the guard posted at their house to make sure he was awake and not snoozing, at least that was how Tom rationalized the anxiety that was making him a nuisance to the sentry doing his job. Between these phone calls he was able to learn that Ludwig's wife, Naomi, was staying at a Chicago hotel while visiting their daughter and Ludwig was not staying with her at the hotel. So the question of the long, sleepless night was where in the U.S. was Ludwig? When he boarded the 6 AM flight to D.C., his exhausted mind told him Ludwig could be anywhere in the world and his wife could have been sent to Chicago as a decoy to distract from his real purpose of visiting the United States.

· · · ·

In his single days Gleason would have gone straight to the office after arriving back in town on a red-eye flight. After his marriage everything changed—so he tried to convince himself. His mind was in a hundred different places as he talked to and dismissed the house guard parked in his car at the curb in front of their house. His long embrace with Cindy still in her night-robe brought him quickly to the present only to be distracted by the welcome smell of coffee wafting into the hallway.

Cindy needed to continue her teaching duties at Catholic University, so Gleason cleared it with his personnel department that an intern, trained in the use of firearms, would shadow her 24/7. She objected to what she felt was this obtrusive coverage, but relented when Tom told her this was only going to be necessary until Ludwig's whereabouts was determined.

When he finally got to his office, his secretary handed him an important memo written in red ink to call a local number. No name, just the number, so he dialed it. "It was him. I realized it after they left. It was one of the damn Nazi brothers. I'll kill him if I see him again."

'The old man is delusional,' Gleason thought to himself.

Before he could respond, Perlman continued. "He was with a young man who's been in the store before looking for old copies of Mein Kampf. Murderers! I'll kill them both."

Gleason asked the question he knew the answer to, "Isaac, who are you talking about?"

"One of the Nazi brothers who betrayed my family. The young man wearing a pea jacket looks just like one of the Nazi brothers from years ago. The older man looked different. His big nose is gone, but his ear is the same."

"His ear's still the same?"

"He has large ear lobes, but the right one does not touch the side of his face. The kids nicknamed him Split-ear. He always tilted his head to the right trying to get his ear lobe to touch his skin. He's still doing it—tilting his head to the right."

"Anything else?"

"His eyes are different colors. One is blue and the other is black. Never saw that before. The Nazis experimented on changing the color of eyes in the concentration camps."

"Did you sell them one of the books?"

They wanted to buy both books, but I told them that I'd only sell one book. As I told you, I need to burn one book to purify my spirit. They said they'd come back in a couple days. I'll kill them when they come back.

"Did the older man recognize you?"

"What difference does that make? I'll kill him before he kills me."

Gleason was impressed with Isaac's bravado, but he would be no match for the younger and stronger man, whom Gleason presumed was Ludwig. "Isaac, I want to help you catch them and we'll let the courts punish them. I'll be over before lunch to talk about this."

After hanging up with Isaac his secretary brought him a couple more items which needed his attention. He knew he should update his boss on everything going on, especially the possibility that Ludwig was in Washington. However, George was out of town for a few days, so Gleason was going to be operating on his own.

The most important information in his stack of notes and faxes that accumulated during his brief trip to Miami was a succinct memo from the Paris Interpol office stating that the subject, Jacob Rosen was a sealed file to the public but still an open investigative file and Interpol must be notified if the whereabouts of Jacob Rosen is known under penalty of law.

'Whose law?' Gleason wondered to himself, as Interpol was an information gathering agency, not an enforcement agency.

Before Gleason could get away to visit Isaac, he took the phone call from the Miami coroner, who described with great clinical dispassion the condition of the corpse found at the eye doctor's office fire. Blunt trauma had fractured the top of victim's skull in an area that a fall could not have caused. The caved-in skull was ruled as cause of death and not the fire, even though the body was burnt beyond recognition and dental records had to be used to positively identify the victim, who indeed was the doctor-owner of the office.

The office building was declared a total loss, and the medical records were likewise a pile of ashes since a hydrocarbon accelerant like gasoline had been poured on them to insure their complete destruction. Gleason asked the coroner to get the medical records from nearby hospitals of any patients this doctor had treated there in the last three years, which was sufficiently long ago to pick-up an unhappy patient. A seriously deranged and disgruntled patient could be responsible for this carnage, and the hospital records were the only place the investigation could look for a clue.

After hearing the details of this professional-style hit, Gleason decided he had better get over to Isaac's bookstore before it was too late. He told his secretary he'd be back after lunch.

XXVI

Since it was lunchtime there were more customers than usual browsing the dusty tables and stacks of the Antiquities Forever store. Nevertheless, Gleason was relieved to see Isaac holding court with his usual banter behind the checkout counter. "I should've called you earlier, but I couldn't find your number. Earlier I sold book eighty-eight to the kid who was in before. He was alone. He paid with this crumpled-up fifty-dollar bill."

Thank God Isaac didn't try to kill the kid as he had threatened, Gleason thought as he reached for the fifty Isaac was holding. After quickly examining it, noticing the serial number was identical to the previous counterfeit bills, Gleason took fifty-dollars from his money-clip and tried to hand it to the demurring Isaac as a trade for the crumpled fifty.

Isaac lowered his hands to his side while shaking his head. "Blood money, I won't take it! I still have book 100 to burn."

Perlman said that the kid was very nervous and was in a big hurry to get back outside to his Dad, who was double-parked waiting for him. Perlman did not know how helpful he had been, as the hidden camera probably captured the car and the small tracking strip that the CIA secreted in the book's binding should allow it to be traced.

The security film was immediately analyzed; there was a good full-face shot of the young man entering Perlman's store. Gleason had a copy printed so he could show his wife to possibly identify him as her stalker. The waiting car that was double-parked was a battered Metro cab with an unidentifiable back-seat passenger. The cab and license plate numbers were readable, so Gleason called his friend, a captain in the D.C. police department, for help in quickly locating the cab.

Within an hour the captain called back with the address where the occupants of the cab were dropped-off, a townhouse in a trendy Georgetown neighbor. Since Gleason was in possession of the counterfeit fifty-dollar bill, he explained he was getting a search warrant from the federal court and would proceed with an arrest that very afternoon. The captain's offer of assistance, especially the closing- off of the street and having a swat team on stand-by, was accepted by Gleason.

Gleason had the bogus fifty-dollar bill in a plastic evidence bag when he walked into the Federal magistrate's office to request a search warrant for the Georgetown address. The magistrate was teasing Gleason how it was hardly worth his time with his very busy schedule to sign this search warrant based on only one counterfeit fifty-dollar bill. Gleason retrieved from his briefcase the other bogus fifties in their evidence envelopes and lined them up in a row in front of the magistrate, who just nodded his head and signed.

A team of six men from the local D.C. Treasury Office was assembled, and Gleason gladly surrendered control of the actual raid to a street-hardened lieutenant, who assured Gleason this raid would be a piece of cake in the ritzy Georgetown neighborhood. The lieutenant laughed at Gleason's suggestion that maybe the Swat team should be the first ones into the townhouse since it was their job to bust down doors.

The lieutenant in charge of the raid said he would be disguised as a postal worker with a special delivery package which needed to be signed for. Their ruse would go so far as having a small postal truck double-parked on the street in front of the house. Gleason could wait inside the mail truck until entry into the house was achieved.

Riding with the lieutenant in the postal van and following the team in one of their fully equipped tactical vans, Gleason smiled at the notion that he now felt like a real cop, prepared for a worst case scenario in his first raid, wearing a helmet and a bullet-proof vest.

Two team members were assigned to guard the rear entrance of the house while the remaining team members would stay near the front as the postman rang the doorbell. From the postal truck Gleason could see a young man open the door and the lieutenant give him a box to keep his hands occupied. The lieutenant's stepping inside the door was the signal for the rest of the team members, including Gleason, to barge in with guns drawn. Gleason compared the young man's appearance with the surveillance photo and concluded he was the same person.

The young man's total surprise at the perfectly executed raid slowly turned to anger as Gleason explained he was being taken into custody for the federal offense of passing counterfeit currency to purchase a book earlier in the day. When Gleason asked where the book was, he was answered with a shrug of the shoulders. Then Gleason showed him a copy of the search warrant, which elicited another shrug.

The street-wise lieutenant had an off-centered nose as proof of trusting and not handcuffing a detainee, so he handcuffed the young man as Gleason and the other agents searched the small townhouse. Initially the team had their guns drawn in case there were any other occupants hiding in closets or under beds. In the top drawer of a bedroom dresser, Gleason found nine more counterfeit fifty-dollar bills, a passport, and some bank account statements along with a few letters from the Dominican Republic. All this was put into an evidence bag to be catalogued back at the office. The purchased copy of Mein Kampf was not found.

Back in the living room where the young man and the lieutenant were maintaining an icy silence, Gleason inquired about the other person in the cab. The young man had obviously been watching a lot of TV police shows as he again refused to answer or even to engage in casual conversation. The lieutenant read the defendant his rights before they headed outside for the ride to the jail lock-up.

The defendant's only comment, "I want an attorney," was answered with a nod of Gleason's head.

. . . .

One of the unintended consequences of what Gleason thought would be a discrete raid to catch a petty counterfeiter in affluent Georgetown was the media attention it was generating. Since the raid happened late Friday afternoon, the suspect would not be arraigned that day but would be held over until Monday. Therefore, Gleason was not at liberty to publicly discuss the case or release the suspect's name. However, the media had no trouble learning the identity of the resident of the raided townhouse and, in true journalistic tradition, splashed his name all-over every news-outlet in the D.C. metropolitan area: Bernardo Walther.

Gleason was sure it would only be a day or two before the media uncovered Bernardo's whole life story, beginning with his birth in Miami, even though he was now a citizen of the Dominican Republic. Gleason's Treasury counterfeiting task force members started to realize all this unsolicited media attention could be beneficial in their efforts to locate Bernardo's father, Ludwig, the real object of their raid. Gleason did not believe Ludwig would allow his son to remain in jail for very long without contacting or assisting him.

The court appointed attorney got Bernardo through the booking procedures and the minimal weekend interrogation sessions, but he was replaced for the Monday arraignment by a partner in one of the District's most prominent law firms. Gleason interpreted this change in Bernardo's legal representation as a sign Ludwig had become aware of his son's arrest and was determined to beat the charge at whatever cost. However, Gleason was shocked when he entered the courtroom and saw an attractive, middle-age woman sitting beside the shackled and handcuffed defendant. While signing the courtroom registration book, he read the name Naomi Walther written on the line above his signature.

These Monday arraignments were usually a rubberstamp formality to clear the jail of the weekend detainees and to set a trail date depending on how the defendants pled to their charges. The prosecutor's request for a ten million-dollar bail caused the judge to sit-up in his chair. After reading the case's paperwork, he looked over the top of his reading glasses at the prosecutor. "The defendant is charged with passing a counterfeit fifty-dollar bill?"

"Yes, your honor."

The judge pounded his gavel and announced that the court would take a fifteen-minute recess while the attorneys convened in his chambers.

"What's this case all about?" the obviously upset judge asked. "I have billion-dollar security fraud cases before me that don't set this high a bail."

"We view the defendant as a flight risk since he is from the Dominican Republic. We have evidence that the counterfeit bill originated there as part of an international money plot," the fidgeting prosecutor said.

"Your honor, please pardon my expression, but this is a bullshit case. The defendant is a graduate student at Georgetown Law School. He got the counterfeit bill as change at a grocery store before he used it to buy a book. This case should be dismissed today." The defense attorney was unaware of or ignored the other counterfeit bills found in the defendant's dresser.

The junior prosecutor knew that his case was in trouble when the defense attorney felt comfortable in using his crude vulgarity in the judge's chambers.

Looking at the nervous young prosecutor and the confidant defense attorney, the judge cracked a smile when he said, "We'll have the court determine if this case is bull-shit or not. However, I am reducing the defendant's bail to one thousand–dollars, and he must surrender his passport and not leave the District of Columbia without the court's permission. Any objections?"

Both attorneys spoke in unison, "No objections, your honor."

After the judge returned to the courtroom and legally formalized the backroom agreement, all the concerned parties adjourned to the spacious outer hallway. Gleason interrupted the defense attorney's huddle with his client and the middle-age woman using the pretense of needing the attorney's business card. While momentarily glancing at the card, he extended his hand toward the woman with the comment, "I feel like I know you since I was given a tour of your Dominican home by your husband."

She didn't reciprocate his handshake and abruptly turned away in a flushed huff with the comment, "So you're the one ruining my son with this false counterfeiting charge."

Before Gleason could respond, the defense attorney used his out-stretched arms to steer his people down the broad marble staircase to the court's business office where he could post the thousand-dollar bail money. Gleason realized this was where they were headed, so he delayed going there to surrender the confiscated passport he had removed from his evidence bag.

Gleason used this little break to set-up a tail on Bernardo and his mother. He told the assigned agents that they were mainly interested in discovering if Ludwig was still in the D.C. area and not so much the activities of the mother and son.

XXVII

The torrential rain falling on the D.C. area brought out the chivalry in Gleason, so he offered to pick-up his wife to spare her the trudge to the Metro station. After a few weeks of marriage he was getting better at reading Cindy's body language, but still his male ego often did not act on this perception. Tonight was different. He could detect by the manner Cindy haltingly approached the car with slouched shoulders while fighting the umbrella in the gusty wind that she needed some quiet time.

He jumped out of the car and met her as she was reaching to open the door. The soggy kiss under the bucking umbrella invigorated both of them. Once in the dry, warm car Tom's proposal of Old Ebbitt's Grill was answered by a dryer and longer kiss. Tom didn't want to sully the makings of a beautiful romantic dinner with his work concerns so before they exited the car at the restaurant, he showed Cindy the surveillance camera photo of the young man he now knew as Bernardo Walther.

"That's him," she said without hesitation. "My stalker!"

'So much for the romantic, candlelight dinner,' he thought. The maître d' at Old Ebbitt's Grill and Tom were on a first name basis because of his frequent business lunches with other up-and-coming Secret Service agents, so he and Cindy were seated in a quiet corner near the table everyone referred to as the White House Secret Service table.

Tom was able to tell Cindy about the day's courthouse drama since it was a matter of public record. They speculated on the whereabouts of Ludwig and how he could just leave his son out there hanging in the breeze with the counterfeiting charge because of the bogus fifty-dollar bill he had given Bernardo to pay for the Mein Kampf book.

The unexpected court-room arrival of Ludwig's wife, Naomi, only generated more questions. Where she had been and how did she even get into the country from her home in the Dominican Republic since she was not a registered passenger on any commercial flight out of the Dominican Republic that Gleason checked?

Cindy was relieved to hear that her stalker was now being stalked by the police-tail Tom had ordered on Bernardo and his mother in the hopes of being led to Ludwig. Tom did not share with Cindy his apprehension that Ludwig could turn into another stalker or worse if he was not located soon.

Tom wanted to get away from his work talk so he asked Cindy about her workday. "Not nearly as exciting as your day in court," she said. "I spent the day in dusty library stacks looking through musty books that haven't been off the shelves in years."

"Sounds like you are researching an obscure topic like a true university professor. You'd make a really good detective if you grow weary of your university research."

"You forget, I hate guns, so scratch that career change idea." Cindy went on to describe the difficulty she was having getting original source material on German-occupied Italy and especially Rome during the 1940's. Fortunately, Rome was spared a lot of the destruction experienced by many of the other Italian cities during the war. "I'm finding that all roads lead to Rome in my quest to link the influence of medieval philosophers to the development of prominent artists of this period as civilization was emerging from the Dark Ages. Unfortunately, much of the art was destroyed or pillaged by the retreating Germans."

As Tom sensed that Cindy was just getting started on her new intellectual pursuit, his not-so-subtle Irish humor drew his hand to his mouth in an attempt to cover a huge yawn. Cindy retaliated by raising her hand to form a pistol pointed at his chest and pulled the trigger. They both laughed and were holding hands when the waiter approached to check on their dessert wishes. "Your research must be uncovering a lot of human drama from the war years besides all the 'old stuff' you are looking for," Tom said in partial appeasement for his insensitivity to Cindy's current intellectual love affair.

"Glad you asked. There is an incident that happened in some caves outside Rome which has me very troubled. I was reading that many of the old valuable art pieces were stashed in caves, castle and monastery basements—anywhere to avoid destruction by the Allied bombing attacks or pillaging by the Germans. One set of caves near Rome did not contain any works of art, but the work of the devil."

Cindy went on to describe what has become known as the Ardeatine Massacre, one of the blackest marks against the occupying Nazi regime in Italy. 335 persons were executed in a series of caves and catacombs outside of Rome where Peter is believed to have met Jesus in a vision.

The massacre in March of 1944 was in retaliation for a terrorist bomb in Rome that killed 33 German soldiers. Hitler ordered that ten Italians must die within 24 hours for every German soldier killed by the bomb. The head of the German occupying forces, Colonel Kettler, was in charge of the gathering the 330 Italian victims, many from jails and prisons who were already facing the death penalty as sentenced by the German-controlled Italian courts. Initially Kettler had trouble reaching his mandated 330 victims and there was some consideration given to picking-up some Jewish victims as Kettler was under orders from Himmler in Berlin to start evacuating the Jews out of Rome to the concentration camps.

The Germany obsession with accurate recordkeeping revealed that indeed 335 victims were killed. The extra 5 victims were prisoners not on Kettler's initial list of 330 who were brought along to the caves at Ardeatine in case they were needed to reach the required number of 330. Once the 330 number was reached, it was decided that since these five extra prisoners had witnessed the massacre they should be taken into the caves and shot.

Cindy paused at this point in her narrative to gather herself, using the napkin to wipe a tear from her eye. Trying to introduce something positive into this depressing story, Tom asked, "Didn't any of the German soldiers object to shooting these helpless victims?"

"One German soldier showed extreme courage and refused to pull the trigger to kill the prisoner kneeling in front of him. Kettler was enraged and found the soldier crying in the cave, still grasping his pistol, which Kettler took and pointed back at the soldier. Instead of shooting the soldier, he steered him at the point of his own pistol back to where another prisoner was kneeling. Kettler held the pistol at the back of the prisoner's head and made the soldier pull the trigger, splattering blood and brains all over the three of them."

Cindy again reached for the napkin to use as a tissue, "That's a terrible story," Tom said. "Where did you read it? Truth can be stranger than fiction."

"The story was in a book on loan from the Vatican Library because of Peter's connection to these caves. Katz was this German soldier's name and he went AWOL from the German army the next day."

Kettler had been over-heard telling one of his Lieutenants that he should have shot Katz for disobeying an order, so initially, after Katz was discovered AWOL, everyone assumed that Kettler had killed Katz. However, in a couple days Kettler went so far as to accuse the Vatican of kidnapping and hiding Katz when he met with the Vatican's Monsignor O'Flaherty outside St. Peter's Square. Kettler suspected O'Flaherty of running a Roman Escape Line that aided fleeing Jewish citizens and escaped Allied prisoners in their quest to get out of the country. He was looking for an excuse to raid the Vatican, but he couldn't get his superiors in Berlin to approve such a bold move.

Even though the Vatican was a neutral sovereign state like Switzerland, Kettler was still desperately looking for any excuse to raid it based on all the rumors circulating around Rome on the Roman Escape Line that Msgr. O'Flaherty was running. If Katz was being given refuge in the Vatican, Kettler would have had the justification that he needed for the raid on the Vatican, even though it would be grossly unpopular with rest of the world.

"Was Katz ever found?" Tom asked.

"Not that I know of. The story ended with Kettler and the Gestapo still looking for him."

XXVIII

The Secret Service tails on Bernardo and his mother did not lead to Ludwig as was Gleason's hope. When Naomi took a cab to Washington National Airport, Gleason had to make a quick decision whether to have the tailing-agent get on the same flight to Miami with Naomi or simply have an agent waiting in Miami to pick up the tail. The intermediate stop at Atlanta worried Gleason since Naomi could get off the plane there and be lost to the world like Ludwig seemed to be.

The lady behind the airline ticket counter commented to the agent, "No bag to check and not even a small carry-on?"

"Going to Miami, travelling light. I'm wearing my bathing suit under my pants."

They both had a good laugh as the agent kept one eye on Naomi finishing her ticketing in another line with a small carry-on but no checked suitcase.

The agent followed Naomi at a discrete distance as she headed for their flight's boarding gate down the long polished terrazzo hallway. At the gate Naomi boarded when the first class passengers were called, whereas the agent's assigned seat was in the rear of the plane, which could be problematic when they landed as Naomi would deplane well before the agent.

• • • •

After Gleason read the multi-page Miami police department fax and got off the phone with the head of the Treasury office in Miami, he felt like he should be on the plane to Miami in place of the tailing-agent. At least he should be there to greet Naomi as she deplaned. It was explained to Gleason that when there was a suspicious unsolved murder in Miami like Dr. Eggert's, a complete background check of the victim was done. This post-mortem background check was more thorough than the pre-sentencing report for a heinous defendant since the victim could no longer speak for himself. Also, it might provide clues to help solve the case. Gleason read that Dr. Eggert had practiced in other Miami locations and he had moved to this location after becoming an eye doctor.

A convenience store's security camera, located across the street from the murdered doctor's burned office, captured a blurred image of a man leaving the medical office a few minutes before the fire was reported. He was carrying what looked like a sawed-off baseball bat or a billy club. The faxed photo image of the man was probably too blurred to be admissible as evidence in court and his car was parked too far up the street to be completely captured by the security camera. Nevertheless, Gleason would have his photo technicians try to work another miracle on these photos.

The Miami police reported that the scorched two-gallon gasoline can found in the charred office was traced to a small hardware store up the street from the destroyed doctor's office. The sales clerk had a good recollection of a recent gas can sale because the customer tried to pay for it with a fifty-dollar bill. The small store didn't have change for the fifty, so the customer paid for it with a combination of smaller bills, complaining in Spanish-accented broken English that now he wouldn't have small bills for his vending machine purchases on the road.

A surprising fact Gleason read in the Miami report was that the deceased Dr. Eggert had moved from the Dominican Republic to Miami after the end of WWII. His application for a Florida Medical License listed him as a 1935 graduate of the University of Berlin Medical School, which was not supported by a copy of his diploma not transcripts of his grades.

When he immigrated to the Dominican Republic from Europe in 1943, Dr. Eggert was immediately granted a license to practice medicine in the DR based on letters of recommendation by a few esteemed medical colleagues in Germany. A cover letter explained that the formal documents of his education in Germany were not available as they were destroyed in the war.

Dr. Eggert's Florida medical license was granted through a credentialing process under the supervision of a state board appointed physician, Dr. Kannon, who was required to scrub in and assist Dr. Eggert performing his first five surgical cases. The Miami police report contained complete copies of these first five surgical cases.

Gleason was pleased to read the very detailed summary report of Dr. Eggert's first case where even the names of the operating room nurses were listed. The first patient, Ludwig Walther from the Dominican Republic, had multiple surgical procedures performed by Dr. Eggert, assisted by Dr. Cannon: a rhinoplasty, bilateral upper and lower eyelid revisions, and scar removal on two sites of the patient's left arm.

Gleason, not being a doctor, still understood the appearance altering results of the two facial procedures, the nose job and reshaping the face around the eyes, but the scar removals on the patient's left arm baffled him. Dr. Eggert's two-week post surgical check-up notes commented that healing was uncomplicated and that he would check the patient periodically back in the Dominican Republic as he returned there for vacations. Lucinda Alverez, patient number five and the final of the required five supervised cases, was also from the Dominican Republic. Her procedure, done a month after Ludwig's surgery, was listed as a bilateral mammary augmentation. Her name did not register with

Gleason until he read the name of her spouse, Carlos. Gleason had not paid any attention to his friend Carlos' last name or the name of his spouse, but now he certainly would have to make another phone call to the Dominican Republic to determine if his friend, Carlos, and Lucinda were husband and wife. In the payment section of Alverez's hospital form, Gleason noted the same letters—PP—as was on Ludwig's form, and he interpreted them to mean—Patient Pay.

Dr. Kannon's office phone number was listed on these old operating reports, so Gleason called it on the odd chance that it was still an active phone number. The receptionist's perky greeting, "Dr. Kannon's office," left Gleason momentarily speechless before he asked to speak to Dr. Kannon.

After Gleason identified himself as an officer of the Department of Treasury investigating the death of Dr. Eggert, he thought he heard Dr. Kannon mumble, 'I knew I shouldn't have accepted that damn supervising job.'

Gleason offered to meet personally with Dr. Kannon rather than engage in a lengthy phone conversation, but it was immediately apparent Dr. Kannon preferred the immediacy and relative anonymity of the phone call. He said that he remembered all five cases of Dr. Eggert, but the first case especially stuck out in his memory. Dr. Eggert had impressed him as a competent surgeon and thus he recommended him to the medical board for his Florida medical license.

He recalled asking Dr. Eggert during the first case how the patient got the scar on the inside of his upper left arm as well as the one on the top side of his left forearm. Dr. Eggert said the upper arm scar was the result of a crude attempt to burn off a tattooed name or letters with multiple cigarette burns many years ago. "Why would someone do this painful self-mutilation?" Dr. Kannon had asked Dr. Eggert.

Without looking up from the surgical site, Dr. Eggert replied, "It was a matter of life and death," without further explanation. Dr. Eggert only performed derma-abrasion with a machine like an electric sander to try to remove the superficial, crudely tattooed numbers on the patient's left forearm. Dr. Eggert anticipated Dr. Kannon's question when he said, "Concentration camp numbers."

After getting over the shock of hearing this reply, Gleason asked Dr. Kannon what he remembered about the fifth surgical case, the breast augmentation of a patient named Lucinda Alverez. After a lengthy pause, Dr. Kannon answered, "The surgical case was routine. Mr. Walther, the first patient, had accompanied the patient and paid for the surgery. She was employed as a maid at his house."

Gleason thanked Dr. Kannon for his information and promised to be in touch if further information was needed.

XXIX

"Do you want to come with me to the library today to start your research on the Ardeatine massacre?" Cindy asked over their morning coffee.

Tom's occasional sharing of morning coffee with Cindy before they headed their separate ways was one of his rationalizations that he was the changed man—less driven and work-obsessed—which Cindy sought as a pre-condition to their marriage. "Is this an invitation to take me into a dark, secluded corner of the stacks?"

"Dream on, lover boy," Cindy teased.

Tom stood and gave Cindy a hearty embrace and a prolonged kiss, not the usual out-the-door, quick peck on the cheek. "Any chance that you could check-out a couple books for me on this massacre?" Tom wondered, obviously by-passing Cindy's open-ended invitation for a little library togetherness.

"Sounds like you're afraid to do real intellectual research with me in the stacks," Cindy again teased while Tom was filling his travel coffee cup.

"We don't have to go to the stacks to do that research if you bring the books home," Tom winked as he was out the door to do his own research at the Antiquities Forever store before going to his office.

Perlman was turning the lights on and preparing the store for its first customer who today happened to be his friend, Gleason.

"Isaac, you mentioned that you thought the young Katz's brothers were in the SS when they stopped by your family printing shop to get a copy of the Mein Kampf?"

Perlman exploded, "Thought! I knew they were in the SS. They were proudly wearing damn SS uniforms." Perlman's chin dropped to hit his chest in reaction to Gleason's traumatic question.

Gleason gave Perlman a few moments to gather himself before he asked, "Are there any records anywhere that would list where the Katz brothers served in the SS during the war?"

Perlman perked up at the chance to be of help in tracking down the traitorous brothers. "The Nazis destroyed a lot of records as the Russians advanced on Berlin. Simon Wiesenthal and other groups have researched many high ranking Nazi officials resulting in the capture of Eichmann in Argentina and in locating Dr. Mengele there, too. The Katz brothers may be too low ranking for Wiesenthal's research, but I know that they were in the SS."

"If they walked in your store today, how could you tell that they were in SS?'

"I'd rip their shirts off and check under their left arms for tattoos of their blood type. This is how many SS criminals were caught trying to escape Germany after the war. Many tried to burn these incriminating tattoos off with cigarettes. But that always left a big scar. They had the nerve to show my father these tattoos when they took their copy of Mein Kampf. "

Gleason was too stunned to reply as he thought back to the report of Dr. Eggert's first surgical case on Ludwig. Finally, he asked, "What about tattoos on left forearms?"

Perlman slowly—almost reverentially—rolled up his left sleeve, "You mean like this," he whispered as he held his arm up for Gleason to see the faded but still readable five numbers. "Permanent remembrances of concentration camps, and this one from my printing work camp. I'm one of the lucky ones who lived to show it."

Gleason gently held Perlman's left hand like a precious religious relic as he slid behind the counter and gave Perlman a long
embrace. "Can someone have both tattoos? A SS member and a
concentration camp survivor?"

Gleason could almost hear the wheels in Perlman brain churn-
ing, searching for an answer to this vexing question. "With the
Nazis and the SS anything is possible—they killed six million of
my people without shedding a tear. A SS member could have tattooed himself with a fake prisoner number to create a Jewish identity to avoid capture after the war and to establish a new life.
Some death-camp survivors have had their tattoos removed to try
to forget what happened. Not me. I never want to forget."

Gleason did not want to share this possible explanation of
Ludwig's double tattoos and probable double life with Perlman
until it was confirmed. Only the unmasking of his treachery could
be properly celebrated.

• • • •

As Gleason made his usual diagonal shortcut to his office across
Lafayette Park passing in front of the White House, he paused
before a group of camped-out protestors urging non-violence and
world peace at any cost. He wondered if any of these protestors
would dare speak on behalf of Hitler's six million victims if the
U.S. hadn't fought in WWII. As he continued his walk to his office
at a reduced, more contemplative pace, he was surprised he did
not feel more elated at solving one of the enigmas surrounding
Ludwig with the help of Perlman's very personal revelation of his
own Nazi prison work camp number. He knew every positive turn
in an investigation usually generated more questions that then
required answers.

The secretary handed Gleason his usual stack of notes and
phone messages with the admonition to read the top one from
the boss who wanted a meeting immediately. Before calling to
set-up the meeting with his boss, Gleason wanted a quiet minute

to assimilate Perlman's thunderbolt with everything else he knew about Ludwig. He needed to mentally prepare before he gave his brief update report to his boss.

The boss's secretary wasted no time in telling Gleason to come upstairs immediately. The urgency in her voice made for a long elevator ride. He wondered what he had messed-up so badly that he was probably being pulled off the Caribbean counterfeit case.

The boss jumped out from behind his desk to greet Gleason as he entered the office. With a hearty handshake he said, "Congratulations, Gleason. You've got it—almost."

Gleason sat down with an obviously bewildered look on his face, so the boss added, "Your promotion to the Presidential Protection Division."

Gleason wasn't often caught speechless but all he could say was, "Really?" The triteness of his reply brought a relieved smile to his face as he had been expecting a dressing-down for some major faux pas in the Caribbean case.

The boss went on to explain that he had again passed all the background checks and was given all the necessary security clearances to be up-close and personal with the highest members of the government, including the Vice-President and the President. Congress was on the verge of passing the necessary appropriation bill to fund the additional slots in the Presidential Protective Division—PPD—so he could expect to start the mandatory training for this promotion to the highest ranks of the Secret Service within two to three months. However, even before that mandatory training, the boss related he was requested to furnish additional agents next week for a special congressional delegation going to the United Nations in New York, so Gleason was volunteered for this role.

The boss magnanimously offered Gleason the chance to use some annual leave for a little vacation before the PPD training started, because the PPD was a notorious vacation killer. Gleason thanked his boss for this offer, but he offered the excuse that Cindy was busy with her teaching schedule and a new research project, so it would be impossible for them to travel anywhere. Gleason did not tell his boss that his main reason for not wanting to use his vacation time was his ongoing involvement in the rapidly expanding counterfeiting case involving Ludwig.

The boss looked at his watch and stood up to escort Gleason to the door, an obvious indication that the meeting was over. Gleason took this as a sign he should continue with his current investigations, except now with more urgency since his days in this department were numbered.

XXX

Gleason was anxious to tell Cindy of his promotion to the PPD, but he resisted the impulse to immediately call her with the good news to allow himself the time to fully assimilate it. He opted for sharing the good news over a nice bottle of wine while savoring Cindy's adventuresome cooking.

Not looking at his secretary's stack of memo's, Gleason knew the first thing he had to do was call the Dominican Republic. Carlos was at his concierge desk and answered after the first ring, "Iberostar, Concierge desk, Carlos speaking."

"Hi, Carlos," Gleason began. "Anything new on Ludwig and his wife?"

"They are both back home here. I was told that they attended Friday's evening synagogue services in Sosua, kind of rare for them."

"Do you have a passport, Carlos?" Gleason abruptly asked, changing the focus from Ludwig to Carlos.

"Si. I need it to visit my sons in Spain and Puerto Rico."

"Your wife must have one also if she goes to visit them with you."

"Si. Hers is under her name of Lucinda Alverez."

"Have you two ever visited the United States?"

Gleason was surprised at the long delay before Carlos replied to this simple question. "Lucinda saw a doctor years ago for surgery.

I couldn't afford to go with her, so a friend went with her."

"When's the last time you have been to the U.S.?"

After an even longer wait, Carlos replied, "My wife and I returned to her doctor in Miami a few years ago to take out the silicon bags that had broken. That surgery, done at Ludwig's suggestion, ruined our lives."

"Was it Dr. Eggert?"

"Si. I thought that he was our friend after we helped him come to the Dominican Republic from Germany. He and Ludwig were friends because he knew something about Ludwig that no one else knew."

"What did Eggert know about Ludwig?" Gleason asked.

"I don't know for sure, but my Dad once said shortly after Ludwig got here that Ludwig was not all Jewish. As a kid, I didn't know or care what that meant."

"Ludwig and Eggert knew each other in Germany, so that could be the secret," Gleason said.

Gleason, listening closely to Carlos' answers, picked up on Carlos' use of 'was, were and did' as if he knew that Dr. Eggert was dead. "Have you been to the U.S. recently?"

"Why would I want to come to the U.S.? I have no money to travel except to see my sons, and my wife hates Miami after what Dr. Eggert and Ludwig did to her there."

Gleason was shocked at the belligerence and hostility in the usually placid Carlos's reply so he asked, "When did Lucinda stop working for Ludwig?"

"A few months after her surgery. He wanted to take pictures of her and she refused. Years later he still calls her, but she won't talk to him."

Gleason's suspicion of Carlos possible killing of Eggert, based on the gasoline can sales clerk's description of a Spanish accented purchaser started to fade as he realized Carlos was more likely to kill Ludwig for trying to seduce his wife than Dr. Eggert for the botched surgery.

"Carlos, you must always let me know if you hear of Ludwig

coming to the U.S. It might solve Lucinda's problem with Ludwig."

Nevertheless, to corroborate Carlos' story, Gleason's next phone call was to their Miami Secret Service office asking them to check the airlines and the Customs and Immigration services for a Carlos Alverez entering and leaving the country a few days before and after Dr. Eggert's murder. Also a check with the rental car agencies about the blurred car image of a Toyota on the security camera near the destroyed office might reveal the name of a possible suspect. Gleason felt increased pressure to bring this Ludwig case to a conclusion after his boss told him of his impending promotion to the PPD, where any further investigation would then be off-limits.

. . . .

When Tom noticed their all-is-good signal—the turned-on porch light—he removed the bottle of Cindy's favorite Pinot Grigio from its brown paper bag. After Cindy accepted it from him while simultaneously giving him a welcome home kiss, she wondered, 'What has he done now?' She pointed into his study off the vestibule where he noticed two thick old books on his desk. "Brought you some homework," she said. "These books are written in English, but there were also other pertinent reference books written in Italian and German."

"Thanks for bringing just the English ones, unless you wanted to spend the evening translating the others for me," Tom said.

"That's not my idea of a romantic evening," Cindy replied as she gave him a gentle push toward the books in his office to keep him out of the kitchen while she prepared dinner.

He found just a few chapters in each yellowing book on the Nazi occupation of Italy and specifically of Rome. The books went on to describe the cat-and-mouse game of helping or capturing war-time escapees played-out between the Vatican's Monsignor O'Flaherty and the Nazi SS Colonel Kettler that was an interesting footnote to the larger war engulfing Europe and, of immediate concern to Gleason, Rome.

Gleason was intrigued by the at-times seemingly contradictory public wartime positions of the Catholic Church headquartered in the Vatican, the smallest sovereign country in the world by virtue of the 1929 Lateran Treaty with Italy. Italy had been conquered and occupied by the Nazi regime, but the 108 acres of the Vatican remained a free and sovereign country with its declared neutrality in WWII, like Switzerland. This legal formality of neutrality certainly was not the impediment that stopped Hitler from invading the Vatican or Switzerland. Neither country was a military threat to him. He needed the Swiss banking structures to help finance his war efforts, and he didn't want to antagonize the sizable German and worldwide Catholic population.

The books confirmed the Roman Escape Line that used a number of Vatican supported safe houses to hide most of the escapees on-the-run from the pursuing Nazis and the ruthless Gestapo. O'Flaherty used his discretion with the more high profile escapees—those most wanted by the Nazis—to give them new identities and quickly hustle them away from Rome, often times to Genoa where they could be put on an ocean-going freighter headed for the diplomatically neutral Spain, out of the Nazi's fatal grasp before sailing to the Americas. This Rome to Genoa to Spain excursion was also a popular escape route for the Jews trying to escape deportation to the concentration camps.

Gleason was reading a long small-print footnote describing the degree of subterfuge the Vatican engaged in to assure the safety of one high profile escapee when Cindy appeared in the study door to announce dinner was ready. He tried speed-reading the small print of the footnote after he shouted to Cindy, "Be right there," but unfortunately he found himself having to slowly reread the footnote to capture its full impact.

"Sorry," he said, as he joined Cindy, who had already started eating. "It's all your fault. You brought the books."

Cindy looked at him, momentarily perplexed. If she didn't know her husband's strange sense of humor, she could have thrown her plate of food at him, or at least left the table. "You're welcome," she smartly replied.

Tom raised his wine glass in a conciliatory toast. "I love you, dear. Your research has solved the Ludwig case, and your cooking is fattening me up for the kill."

Tom went on to explain the workings of the Vatican's Roman Escape Line. One of their proudest works was the change of identity of a Nazi soldier, Ernst Katz, who refused to participate in the Ardeatine Cave massacre outside Rome. Whereas, while working under Colonel Kettler, the soldier Katz had been trying to entrap and capture Msgr. O'Flaherty for his work on the Roman Escape Line, he later sought O'Flaherty's protection in the Vatican to escape Kettler, who had threatened to send him back to Germany for a court marshal for disobeying his shooting order, which came directly from Hitler.

The Vatican was always suspicious of every refugee who came knocking on their door seeking asylum, because one turncoat could put hundreds of refugees' lives at risk. When the arrival of Katz at the Vatican became known to O'Flaherty, he immediately interviewed him to ascertain the sincerity of his coming to the Vatican for asylum. As a reference Katz gave O'Flaherty the name of their family banker in Geneva, who also did business with the Vatican. Once this Swiss banking reference verified Katz's family identity, the overly trusting O'Flaherty heard and believed Katz's Ardeatine Cave massacre story where he refused to killed the helpless prisoners. With Kettler leaving no stone unturned searching for Katz, O'Flaherty did not have the means nor the time to investigate Katz's earlier war career in Germany. He knew Katz had to be moved quickly out of the Vatican as Col. Kettler would turn Rome and the defenseless Vatican upside-down to find his treacherous aide.

O'Flaherty calculated Katz would have a better chance of getting out of Rome and Italy if he was perceived as an escapee from a German concentration camp rather than if he was discovered as a runaway, deserting German soldier, so five numbers were crudely tattooed on Katz's left forearm with a needle and black ink. The real prison camp tattoos were put on with a specially developed electric tattoo machine and were driven deeper under the skin than Katz's more superficial one. Katz was given new identity papers with the name of Ludwig Walther. The footnote in Cindy's research book ended with the statement that Katz, now named Ludwig Walther, was last seen standing at an ocean-going freighter's railing as it sailed from Genoa's Harbor to Spain.

After listening to Tom's narrative, Cindy had no one but herself to blame for Tom's ramblings since she had brought the books home. Finally she asked, "Are you sure that this Katz is now the Ludwig Walther that you are investigating?"

"I'm as sure as you can be in these investigations. There are probably other sources, like the sealed Vatican archives that I can try to access to get more information. The Pope was reported to have buried his face in his hands when he was informed of the cold-blooded Ardeatine massacre, so the Vatican was surely aware of it. Want to take a quick trip to Rome for more research after I get back from New York?"

"New York?"

Tom had been so self-absorbed in his own investigative world that he had neglected to tell Cindy about the most important news of the day, if not of their recently married lives, his promotion to the PPD. "Oh, my God, Cindy! Please forgive my total absorption in the task at hand. My boss told me today I have been promoted to the Presidential Protective Division. Rather than interrupt your research with a call today, I wanted to tell you in person over this wonderful dinner."

The special bottle of wine now made sense to Cindy. She leaned across the table to give Tom a celebratory kiss. "Congratulations, dear—looks like our lives will be changing."

XXXI

Gleason was so preoccupied with his unraveling of the Ludwig Walther enigma that his orders for his first PPD assignment as a member of the Congressional Protective Division, CPD, snuck up on him more quickly than he thought they would. He was ordered to report to the suburban Andrews Air Force for the flight to New York with the Congressional Delegation headed for the United Nations. The Speaker of the U.S. House of Representatives is in line after the President and Vice President for succession to the U.S. Presidency so the Secret Service is required to provide the Speaker of the House with protection, especially when in a potentially threatening environment like the United Nations in New York.

The other members of the Congressional Delegation in New York would be under the broad umbrella of the CPD, but not subject to or eligible for the same 24/7 coverage as the Speaker of the House. There were two rookie Secret Service agents, Gleason and an agent assigned from the Treasury Department's New York office, on this United Nations assignment. Gleason was aware that the rookies were on the bottom of the totem pole so they could expect to do the things the senior agents chose not to do.

The ever-vigilant agents mingled with the senators and congressmen at the cocktail parties and receptions that seemed to

overshadow the formal meetings at the United Nations. Gleason
was especially impressed by a gregarious young southern congressman and his wife Kathy, who were busily working the cocktail party crowd introducing their short-in-stature friend with a
strange sounding name, Azee. The Secret Service agents from the
first day of their training were instructed not to develop any likes
or dislikes of the people that they were protecting, lest it give them
even only a momentary pause in jumping in to stop a bullet meant
for their protectee. Another Secret Service mantra was never to
question any request from their protectee.

As a matter-of-fact, Gleason felt honored that this young
congressman asked him, a rookie on his first protective division
assignment, to stop at a drug store on the way back to the hotel
and pick-up an Akron Tourist Tube for his wife, Kathy. Not wanting to show his ignorance of the Akron Tourist Tube, Gleason
agreed to do as the congressman asked. Gleason thought it a little
strange when his boss broke out into a big smile when Gleason
asked for permission to pick-up the Akron Tourist Tube for the
congressman's wife. The boss told him to take the other rookie
agent with him since he was from New York and might know
where the nearest drug store was.

The two agents were happy to find a drug store only a block
from the congressman's hotel. Gleason asked the first clerk they
encountered where they might find an Akron Tourist Tube.
After repeating a couple times what they wanted, the young
clerk shrugged her shoulders and motioned for them to follow
her toward the pharmacy department in the back of the store.
After shooing the young clerk away, a grey-haired pharmacist
approached the two rookie agents. "You guys look too young to
know the name Akron Tourist Tubes."

Gleason gave a puzzled look to his rookie partner as he spoke
to the pharmacist, "Is this something illegal? We're bringing it
back to a friend's wife."

After muffling his laughter, the pharmacist asked, "What's
Akron known for?"

"Car tires," Gleason answered.

"Made of what?" the pharmacist asked, barely suppressing a smile.

"Rubber," the agents answered in unison as they turned beet-red realizing their own gullible stupidity.

"Take her this," the pharmacist said as he rang-up a small foil package with a circular indentation.

The agents had a good laugh at their trusting naiveté as they turned the corner toward the hotel. "Our boss and the southern Congressional Representative must have been in on this rookie initiation rite," Gleason commented.

"Quite a right of passage," the usually self-assured New York agent said to Gleason as he recognized their boss standing at the hotel's check-in-desk. "Do you want to give this package to the representative's wife?" the New York agent said with a forced straight face.

"You guys keep it as a souvenir of your induction into the big leagues," their boss said as he gave them a pat on their backs for a job well done.

Kathy approached Gleason after lunch the next day and offered her hand to extend an apology. "Sorry about that little rite of initiation yesterday. It seems to be a male thing with my husband trying to entrap the new agents."

"After getting over the initial embarrassment in the drug store we had a good laugh. Nevertheless, tell your husband that pay-backs are hell."

"I would encourage you to repay him with a vengeance," Kathy said as she gave Gleason a quick hug.

While the Congressional Delegation was having its final afternoon session inside the U.N., the two rookies were assigned to the outside courtyard overlooking the murky East River, watching for any danger approaching by water. On his court-yard patrol Gleason passed many times around the cast plowshare that bore the poignant plaque, very apropos for the U.N.: 'Let them beat their swords into plowshares.' He cynically thought if this had happened he would not be chasing Ludwig for his involvement in a World War that would not have been fought. He might may not even have his new job in the PPD.

On his lunch break he found a pay phone outside the basement cafeteria and called his secretary for any messages awaiting his attention. The two important ones that got his attention when she quickly read through the list were one from the Interpol headquarters in Paris requesting a return call and another call from Carlos in the Dominican Republic stating that Ludwig was preparing to leave for the United States. Gleason could not deal with either of these calls on his short lunch break because he did not want to give the appearance of neglecting the day's important CPD duties in favor of his old job responsibilities. They would have to wait until his return to D.C.

Since his rookie partner stayed behind in New York when the congressional contingent returned to Washington, Gleason tried to keep his head below the radar screen on the return flight to Andrew's Air Force base, hoping to avoid any more initiation rituals. When the Air Force pilot announced they were beginning their final descent into Andrew's, Gleason thought he was home-free until the gregarious southern congressman grabbed a microphone from the Air Force steward and asked Gleason to stand up. Gleason looked around for an escape parachute so he could put to use some of his former Navy training. Fortunately, the final initiation rite only consisted of the whole plane singing a round of, 'When Irish Eyes are Smiling,' followed by a robust hand-clap that Gleason responded to with a smiling politician's wave.

XXXII

The duties of Gleason's first CPD assignment ended when the limousine dropped off the Speaker of the House at the House Office Building, a few blocks from Gleason's office in the Treasury Building. Even though most of the staff would have left for the day, Gleason felt the need to go to his office to catch up on everything that happened during his overnight assignment in New York.

As expected, his secretary had left a neat stack of notes and memos he needed to deal with, especially the two he was already aware of: the Interpol call and the message from Carlos. There also was a fax from the Miami police department that a name recovered and restored from under an erased and smudged name on one of Dr. Eggert's medical records was Katz. Since it would be after midnight in Paris, the Interpol call would have to wait until the next morning. However, with the Dominican Republic's time zone only an hour different than D.C. time, he decided to call Carlos with the hope he would still be at his concierge desk.

Carlos answered Gleason's call, but quietly asked him to call back in 15 minutes when he could talk. This short break gave Gleason a chance to focus on other material in his stack of items, the most salient of which was the lab report on the two empty bottles of Presidente beer that Gleason had brought back from the Dominican Republic. The report on the bottle that he had labeled—'Carlos'—stated, "NO MATCH FOUND. The report on the other bottle labeled—'Ludwig'—stated two names, Ludwig Walther and Jacob Rosen, both names recovered from the immigration service's file of frequent travelers to the United States. Gleason shook his head in amazement at how Ludwig, using two different names, was able to come and go in his international travels without being detected.

Carlos picked-up Gleason's second call on the first ring and apologized for not being able to talk earlier because his boss was hovering over his desk. Carlos also apologized for not getting back sooner to Gleason with the news that Ludwig and his wife had already left for America. They had expressed hatred and anger at Gleason because he had set-up their son's arrest for the counterfeiting charge. Ludwig had asked Carlos if he had been in contact with Gleason. Carlos said there had been no contact between them. Carlos could not give any specific flight information on Ludwig's travel except that they left the Dominican Republic on the private plane from the small airport near Puerto Plata.

Gleason knew that tomorrow he would have to try to track down this clandestine flight of Ludwig, but tonight he would have to get home to an already-late dinner with Cindy. He tried to call Cindy, but she didn't answer his call, which was unusual as there was a phone and answering machine on her little desk in the corner of the kitchen. He left a brief message that he was heading home and would be there as quickly as the Metro could bring him. Leaving his office he noticed a light in an office down the hall, so he headed that way to turn it off. Surprisingly, he found Agent Billups closing his briefcase, getting ready to head home also. "Hi, Gleason. I have the car today. Can I take you home?"

"I'd appreciate that. Sure beats the smelly Metro."

The worst of the D.C. rush hour traffic was over as the two agents had a chance to unwind from their busy days. Billups congratulated Gleason on his promotion to the PPD, and Gleason commented he still had a number of things to finish before leaving this department. Gleason jokingly mentioned any unfinished busi-ness, especially the Caribbean counterfeiting case, could very well end-up on Billups' desk.

As the car turned onto his street, Gleason could see lights inside the house, even in an up-stair's bedroom, but no porch light was turned on.   Billups was starting to slow down when Gleason shouted, "Don't stop! Keep driving!" At the first intersec-tion Gleason pointed to the right for Billups to turn. Halfway up the street, where the narrow alley came out, Gleason motioned to park at the curb.

"What's this all about?" a puzzled Billups asked.

"Probably nothing. It's just that Cindy and I have this signal to turn on the outside porch light when we get inside if all is okay—changing neighborhood, you know. She's home and the porch light is not on—the first time this has happened."

Billups, who lived in the suburbs with his wife and three kids, was somewhat confused by Gleason's inner city paranoia, but he was willing to give Gleason the benefit of the doubt because of his changing neighborhood status.

"The other thing that doesn't add–up is that Cindy didn't answer my call before I left the office, as she always does. So some-thing is wrong. You've got your gun, right?"

"Never without it."

"Okay, here's the plan. Leave the car here and we'll walk up the alley. You proceed around to the street and start walking toward the house like you are coming from the Metro."

"Should I have my gun drawn?"

"Hold it in your coat pocket out of sight. It's dark enough that you can pass for me approaching on the street."

"I have one vest in the trunk. You put it on," Billups offered.

"You wear it. Your kids need you." This comment struck home with both of them as Billups opened the trunk to retrieve the bul-letproof vest. Their Secret Service training instructed them to use lethal force only as a last resort, but when the life of a family mem-ber is threatened, the rules become a little more flexible.

As they walked in the shadows of the alley toward Gleason's backdoor, the plan developed. "If there's someone in there with Cindy, he'll be expecting me to come in the front door, but I'm going to quietly enter the basement back door. Let's synchronize our watches so that in exactly five minutes you ring the front door bell and quickly—I mean very quickly—get off the porch and hide in the bushes. Let's assume that the intruder has a gun, so move fast."

"I'm sure glad I'm here to help you. Let's hope that Cindy just forgot to turn on the porch light."

"She never forgets. Something is wrong," Gleason said.

Gleason gave Billups three minutes to make his way out of the alley to the street before he inserted his key into the basement door lock. He thanked his chronic procrastination that he never got around to installing a deadbolt on this basement back door as it would have prevented his stealthy entrance into his home. The door opened with only a slight squeak of the seldom-used hinges. He heard no TV sound from the kitchen above, which was Cindy's constant kitchen companion. With drawn gun he inched his way into the basement using the sliver of light coming under the door at the top of the stairs. He heard a muffled noise coming from a pile of dirty clothes next to the washer and dryer. He dropped to his knees and peeled away a layer of towels and sheets to find Cindy, bound with nylon ties, her mouth covered with duct tape. Whispering to be quiet as he ripped off the duct tape and used his pocketknife to cut off the nylon ties, he heard the faint ring of the doorbell. He helped Cindy to her feet and pushed her out the basement door with the noisy bang of the door behind her.

He heard the front door open and loudly slam shut in obvious frustration that no one was there on the porch. The door to the basement flew open with the person at the top of the stairs perfectly back-lit in the bright hallway.

"Drop your gun and get your hands up, Ludwig," Gleason shouted from behind the wash machine. Two shots rattled through the metal door of the dryer as Ludwig fumbled to find the basement light switch at the top of the stairway. Gleason shouted the warning again as Ludwig again aimed his pistol toward the pile of clothes by the dryer. Before Ludwig could pull the trigger again, two simultaneous shots rang out, and Ludwig was tumbling and bouncing down the stairs like a rampaging rock in a rockslide. Gleason's bullet shattered Ludwig's right knee and Billups' shot in Ludwig's back propelled him head over heels down the stairs.

Billups called to Gleason from the hallway at the top of the stairs, "Gleason, are you alright?"

Looking at Ludwig's unmoving mass at his feet, Gleason hollered back to Billups that the situation was stable and to come downstairs. Gleason ran outside to find Cindy slumped against the basement wall in a state of shock.

He sat down beside her and held her in a long embrace until they could hear the approaching sirens getting closer. Finally, with Tom's assistance, she slowly stood up and they headed back inside together. Billups had covered Ludwig's body with a sheet from the pile of dirty laundry. Gleason pulled back a corner of the sheet exposing Ludwig's head. He bent down and noticed that Ludwig's right ear lobe was not attached to the side of his face just like Perlman had described it.

Billups saw the sheet moving up-and-down and shouted, "He's still breathing," as the first EMT rushed in the basement door.

XXXIII

Cindy and Tom took the next day off-of-work and decided to leave their house since the D.C. Police department, the F.B.I. and the Secret Service all wanted access to their home to conduct their own investigation of the shooting scene. Unless the gravely wounded Ludwig died, Gleason's home was not a homicide site. However, it might as well have been one based on the meticulous care going into all the investigations.

As they were leaving in the morning for their mental health day-trip to Annapolis, Gleason tried to lighten the pall hanging over everyone, especially Cindy, by commenting to the large D.C. patrolman who was appointed to guard the house for the day, "Don't steal any of our sterling silver. Cindy has it all counted."

The cop's quick reply, "You have insurance, don't you?" brought a smile to everyone's face, even Cindy's.

Even though Gleason did not attend the Naval Academy at Annapolis prior to his years in the Navy, he found it a place of refuge and peace to escape the pressures inside the Beltway. There always seemed to be a predictable pace and rhythm of life at the academy that was not present in his current job and certainly would not be present in his new White House assignment. Unfortunately, he didn't have the heart to tell Cindy, after yesterday's near-death experience, that these pressures would be amplified even more after he switched to the PPD. Tom felt responsible for the previous evening's traumatic experience, so he wanted to explain to Cindy all the background leading up to it over a quiet lunch at their favorite Annapolis restaurant, Carrol's Creek.

"It's hard to believe this whole mess started at our wedding and honeymoon," Cindy rather dolefully commented while waiting for their first glass of wine. "And it could have ended a few weeks later in our Washington home."

Tom held her hands across the table to quiet her emotions. "It did end in our home. It's done. An evil man, whether he lives or dies, can never again harm anyone."

Epilogue

The German government petitioned the World Court at the Hague for the release of their fugitive citizen, Ernst Katz, from United States custody. The German government argued that he was an escaped World War II war criminal responsible for numerous atrocities, including homicides, while stationed as an SS officer at Aplerbach, a children's mental hospital, in Dortman, Germany. The United States acceded to this request, reserving the right to prosecute Ludwig Walther for counterfeiting United States currency and attempted homicide at a later date.

Acknowledgments

The publishing of A DOMINICAN REPUBLIC WEDDING completes the Gleason trilogy of exciting stories narrated in THE FIRST LADY SLEEPS and THE FIRST LADY MEETS AZEE. I thank the loyal readers of my previous books for being a continuing stimulus to complete this current book.

Special thanks are due to Frances Schattenberg, Ph.D. who has been a patient mentor bring out the very best in the complex narrative of the unfolding Dominican Republic wedding story. Her keen sense of 'what works' developed over thirty years of university creative writing teaching has faithfully guided me.

The imput of the early readers of the manuscript served as a source of unfailing advice and suggestions. These include Kathy and John Snider, Don Scofield, Roger Rapoport and Msgr. R. Louis Stasker. Sisters, Jane Humphrey and Janet French, were a formidable one-two punch in the final pre-printing stages of the manuscript preparation.

Amy Cole of JPL Design Solutions has done her usual stellar text layout and cover design work. She is a pleasure to work with as she brings the manuscript and the cover alive as a real book. Steve Demos, M.D. used his graphic arts skills to sharpen my cover photo of the Dominican Republic beach wedding scene.

Finally, I express my deep appreciation to my wife, Barb, our four children and their families for their support and encouragement of my writing efforts.

The following bibliography is provided in recognition of the authors, who by their writings have kept alive the memory of one of humanity's darkest hours—the holocaust.

Bibliography

Arnold-Foster, Mark. *THE WORLD AT WAR*. New York, NY, The New American Library, Inc., 1974.

Bascomb, Neal. *HUNTING EICHMANN*. New York, NY, First Marine Books, 2010.

Bongino, Dan. *LIFE INSIDE THE BUBBLE*. Washington, D.C. WND Books, Inc. 2013

Cornwall, John. *HITLER'S SCIENTISTS*. New York, NY, Penguin Group, 2003.

Friedlander, Saul. *NAZI GERMANY AND THE JEWS 1933-1944*. New York, NY, Harper Collins, 2009.

Halbrook, Stephen P. *THE SWISS AND THE NAZIS*. Havertown, Pa, Casemate, 2010.

Hugh, Matthew and Chris Mann. *INSIDE HITLER'S GERMANY*. New York, NY, MJF Books, 2000.

Lifton, Robert Jay. *THE NAZI DOCTORS*. New York, NY, Basic Books, 2000.

Matthews, John W. *BONHOEFFER: A BRIEF OVERVIEW OF THE LIFE AND WRITINGS OF DIETRICH BONHOEFFER*. Minneapolis, Mn. Lutheran University Press, 2011.

Melanson, Philip H. with Peter B. Stevens. *THE SECRET SERVICE*. New York, NY, MJF Books, 2002.

Michener, James A. *CARIBBEAN*. New York, NY, Ballentine Books, 1989.

Nichol, John, and Tony Rennel. *THE LAST ESCAPE*. New York, NY, The Penguin Group, 2002.

Potok, Chaim. *WANDERINGS*. New York, NY, Fawcett Crest Books, 1978.

Reese, Laurence. *AUSCHWITZ*. New York, NY, Public Affairs TM, 2005.

Roland, Paul. *THE NAZIS AND THE OCCULT*. New York, NY, Chartwell Books, Inc., 2010,

Roland, Paul. *THE NUREMBERG TRIALS*. New York, NY, Chartwell Books, Inc., 2010.

Shirer, William L. *THE RISE AND FALL OF THE THIRD REICH*. New York, NY, Simon and Schuster, 1960.

Walker, Stephen. *HIDE AND SEEK*. London, UK, Harper Collins Publishers, 2011.

Walters, Guy. *HUNTING EVIL*. New York, NY, Random House, 2009.